The Restaurant of Lost Recipes

The Restaurant of Lost Recipes

HISASHI KASHIWAI

Translated by Jesse Kirkwood

G. P. PUTNAM'S SONS
New York

PUTNAM
— EST. 1838 —

G. P. PUTNAM'S SONS
Publishers Since 1838
An imprint of Penguin Random House LLC
penguinrandomhouse.com

Copyright © 2014 by Hisashi Kashiwai
Translation copyright © 2024 by Jesse Kirkwood

First published in the United Kingdom by Mantle, an imprint of
Pan Macmillan, 2024.

Originally published in Japanese as *Kamogawashokudo Okawari* by Shogakukan,
Tokyo, Japan.

English edition arranged with Shogakukan through Emily Books Agency, LTD, and
Casanovas & Lynch Literary Agency S.L.

The right of Hisashi Kashiwai to be identified as the author of this work has been
asserted by him in accordance with the Copyright, Designs and Patents Act 1988.

Hardcover ISBN: 9780593717790
eBook ISBN: 9780593717806

Printed in the United States of America
1st Printing

Book design by Ashley Tucker
Title and half title page art by DiViArt/Shutterstock
Knife ornament by Tartila/Shutterstock

CONTENTS

The **Restaurant** of **Lost Recipes**

Chapter 1

Nori-ben

1

Kyosuke Kitano jumped off the Keihan express at Shichijo station, walked up the stairs and out into daylight, then stopped to gaze at the swirling waters of the Kamogawa. It had been five years since he'd moved from the southern prefecture of Oita to nearby Osaka, and yet this was his first trip to Kyoto.

Slung over his shoulder was a navy sports bag printed with the name of his university, its straps digging into his upper arm. Tiny rivers of sweat were running down his muscular neck, leaving damp patches on his white polo shirt. Squinting against the sunlight bouncing off the river, he looked down at the map in his hand and began walking west.

After crossing a bridge, he reached Kawaramachi-dori, where he stopped and began rotating the map this way and that, swiveling on the spot as he did so. He glanced around, rocking his head from side to side in hopeless confusion.

Noticing a man cycling past with a wooden box of the sort used for food deliveries, he called out: "Excuse me! Which way is Higashi Honganji temple?"

"Straight that way," replied the man, pointing west. "Take a right down Karasuma-dori." He began pedaling off.

"It's actually a restaurant on Shomen-dori I'm looking for," said Kyosuke, jogging to keep up.

The man set his feet down from the pedals again. "Mr. Kamogawa's place?"

"Yes, that's the one." Kyosuke showed the man his map. "The Kamogawa Diner."

"Third right, then the second left. It's the fifth building on the left." With these brisk words, the man cycled off.

"Thank you!" shouted Kyosuke, bowing as low as he could to the departing figure. Counting the streets on his fingers, he followed the man's directions until he arrived at his destination: a two-story building with a slightly drab mortar exterior and no sign advertising its presence. It was all just as he'd been told. Kyosuke put a hand to his chest, took three deep breaths, then slid the door open.

"Hello?" he called into the interior.

"Ah," said Nagare Kamogawa, looking up from the counter he was scrubbing. "Come on in."

Kyosuke was somewhat taken aback by this welcoming tone. "I'm . . . here to request your food detective services," he stammered.

"You can relax, you know. I don't bite. Go on, take a seat." Nagare gestured toward one of the red folding chairs at a nearby table.

"Thank you." Kyosuke breathed a sigh of relief, though there was still something vaguely robotic about the way he seated himself on the chair.

"You hungry?" asked Nagare. "How about some grub?"

"Oh . . . you mean I can . . . eat here?" Kyosuke was struggling so much to get the words out that he seemed on the verge of biting his own tongue.

"You might as well, seeing as you're here! Then, afterward, you can tell us about this dish you're looking for."

"You're a student, then?" asked Nagare's daughter, Koishi, emerging from the kitchen just as her father entered it. She wore a sommelier apron over her white shirt and black jeans. "You look like you're in some kind of sports club. Let me guess: kendo. No—judo?"

"Not exactly," said Kyosuke, smiling.

"But those *muscles* . . ." she said, eyeing his biceps. "It must be *some* kind of martial art, right?"

"It's nothing that impressive." Kyosuke accepted a glass of iced tea and began crunching away at the ice cubes.

"Is your university in Kyoto?"

"No, Osaka. Do you know Kindai Sports University? I'm Kyosuke, by the way," he added, getting to his feet as he introduced himself.

"I feel like I've seen you before somewhere. . . ." said Koishi, carefully studying his features.

"Probably just one of those faces," he replied with a shy grin.

"How did you find out about this place, then?"

"Well, see, I live at the university dormitory, and that's where I eat all my meals. I got chatting with the cook about this dish I ate when I was little, and he tried making it for me. But it didn't quite taste the same. When I told him as much, he said I should come here instead. Showed me your ad in *Gourmet Monthly*."

"Ah, the ad," said Koishi, carefully wiping down the table.

Nagare reappeared with a metal tray. It was laden with small dishes. "This probably won't be enough for a youngster like you," he murmured as he set it on the table. "You'll have to let me know if you need seconds."

"This looks . . . incredible," said Kyosuke, gazing excitedly at the food.

"Tsuyahime rice from Yamagata—extra-big portion of that. Pork miso soup on the side. Plenty of root vegetables in there too, even if they're not all fancy Kyoto specialties. Now, the large platter is a fusion of Japanese and Western cuisine. That there is deep-fried hamo eel with sour plum pulp and perilla leaf. The Manganji peppers are deep-fried too. Try those with my homemade Worcestershire sauce. The small bowl is miso-simmered mackerel with a shredded myoga ginger dressing. The roast beef is Kyoto stock—best enjoyed with a drizzle of the wasabi-infused soy sauce and wrapped in a sheet of toasted nori. As for the teriyaki-style duck meatballs, you can dip those in the accompanying quail egg yolk. Chilled tofu garnished with the minced skin of the hamo eel and, finally, deep-fried Kamo eggplant with a starchy curry sauce. Enjoy!"

Kyosuke licked his lips, nodding along enthusiastically to Nagare's every word.

"The food isn't always this fancy, you know," said Koishi with a wink. "Dad got all excited when he saw we had an eligible young bachelor visiting, and now he's pulling out all the stops."

"Shush, you!" said Nagare, dragging her into the kitchen.

For all his enthusiastic nodding, Kyosuke had almost no idea what any of the food in front of him was. Hamo and mackerel were types of fish, he knew that much. But as for what they might taste like . . . The mention of roast beef, Worcestershire sauce, and curry had come as a relief, but even those parts of the meal looked suspiciously different from anything he normally ate.

After ten seconds or so of silent contemplation, he gripped the bowl of rice firmly in his left hand, reached for one of the duck meatballs with his chopsticks, dipped it in the small bowl of quail egg yolk, set it on his rice, then popped it into his mouth.

He let out a quiet gasp of delight, then immediately began working his way through the deep-fried eel and roast beef, his chopsticks working at lightning speed. Every mouthful triggered a murmur of appreciation.

In all honesty, having never eaten anything he could even compare it to, Kyosuke had no way of knowing what standard of cuisine he was eating. What he did know, instinctively, was that the dishes in front of him gave off the same aura as the world's top athletes. The food filling his mouth right now was simply sensational.

"How is it?" asked Nagare, appearing at his side with a glass pitcher of iced tea.

"I don't really know how to describe it. I mean, I know next to nothing about food. But that was an amazing meal."

"Glad to hear it," said Nagare, pouring the tea. "Cooks like me only get one shot at winning over the customer. If they don't like what I serve them, they won't be coming back. Of course, if they do, I get to do it again and again."

Kyosuke sank into thought, as though pondering the significance of Nagare's words.

"If that's filled you up," he continued, "let me show you to the office in the back. My daughter will interview you there."

"Yes, about that . . ." said Kyosuke, draining his glass of tea. "I was just thinking that maybe I don't need your help after all."

Nagare poured him a refill. "Why? That's what you came here for, isn't it?"

"It's just . . ." said Kyosuke, fiddling with his glass. "After eating a meal like that, my own request feels a bit silly."

"Listen. You came to us because you wanted our help re-creating a meal. Something deep inside you told you to come here—something you can't quite put your finger on. A sort of . . . fog inside you. Are you telling me that fog has cleared away completely?"

"But . . ." replied Kyosuke without looking up. "The dish I want help with is so basic I don't even know if you can call it a 'dish.'"

Nagare looked steadily at him. "I don't know what it is you're after, but I can assure you that there's no such thing as 'basic' when it comes to cooking."

Kyosuke nodded deeply, patted his cheeks, then got to his feet.

"All right, then. I'm in."

Nagare smiled. "Glad to hear it. Follow me." He showed Kyosuke toward the door at the back of the restaurant.

"What are these?" asked Kyosuke, glancing at the photos lining the walls of the corridor.

"Dishes I've cooked over the years, mainly," said Nagare.

Kyosuke's eyes darted from one photo to another as he walked. "You really can cook anything, can't you?"

Nagare stopped and turned. "'Jack of all trades and master of none' would be another way of putting it. If I'd focused on just one dish, maybe I'd have earned myself a Michelin star by now."

"Just one dish, eh?" murmured Kyosuke. He had come to a halt and was gazing pensively up into the air.

"You all right?" asked Nagare.

"Oh, I'm fine," said Kyosuke as they began striding down the corridor again.

Koishi was waiting in the office at the back of the restaurant.

"Please—take a seat."

"Right, then." Kyosuke bowed, then settled in the middle of the sofa opposite her.

"Could you fill this out?" asked Koishi, handing him a clipboard with a form on it. "Don't sweat the details."

"My handwriting's terrible. I hope you can read it." He began scribbling away, cocking his head to one side every now and then as if to think.

"Kyosuke Kitano. Kindai Sports University . . ." Koishi clapped her hands. "Now I remember!"

"Remember what?" asked Kyosuke, somewhat bewildered.

"You're that swimmer! I saw you in a magazine. They said you were one of the big hopes for the future." Koishi's eyes were gleaming.

"Oh, I don't know about that," said Kyosuke, smiling modestly as he returned the clipboard.

"You're going to be in the Olympics, aren't you?" asked Koishi, her eyes scanning the rest of the form.

"Depends how I do in the qualifiers."

"It said in the magazine you were a real all-rounder. Freestyle, backstroke—the whole package."

"Actually, people keep telling me I should focus on just one stroke."

"Well, we'll be rooting for you." Koishi pursed her lips. "So, what's this dish you're looking for?"

"I can't believe I'm asking you this," said Kyosuke, dropping his voice and looking down at his feet, "but I'd like you to make me a nori-ben."

"Nori-ben? You mean like . . . the bento box? Nori seaweed on a bed of rice, with deep-fried fish or chikuwa tempura or something on the side?"

"No, nothing on the side." Kyosuke's voice was even quieter now. "Just the nori on the rice."

"Just the nori?" asked Koishi, leaning forward. "Nothing else?"

"That's right," murmured Kyosuke, his muscular body hunching in on itself. His voice was practically a whisper now.

"I'm guessing you didn't eat this at . . . a restaurant, did you?" asked Koishi, peering curiously at him.

"My dad made it for me."

"Your dad's bento, eh . . . Well, why don't you just ask him? If you're from Oita, that's not *too* far away, is it?"

"I haven't spoken to my dad in over five years," said Kyosuke, his voice cracking slightly.

"I . . . see. Do you at least know where he lives?"

"I heard he was living over in Shimane."

Koishi's eyes widened in surprise. "Shimane? Why?"

"Dad was addicted to gambling. That's why Mum walked out on him. Even when he got sick, he insisted the medical fees were a waste of money. Spent all the money we had on keirin racing instead. I guess he's paying the price for all that now. I heard he's crashing at my aunt's place in Shimane while he finally gets treated for his illness."

"Right, then," said Koishi, scribbling something in a notebook. "What about your mum?"

"Remarried. She lives in Kumamoto now."

"And when did she leave your dad?"

"It was the first summer holiday after I started at Oita Junior High, so about ten years ago. Dad bet all the money she'd been saving for a family holiday on a horse race. My little sister went to live with her, but I chose to stay with Dad. Didn't think he'd manage on his own, you see."

"So it was just you and your dad at home, then," said Koishi, turning to the next page of her notebook. "What was his job?"

"He drove a tourist taxi around Oita." Kyosuke smiled bitterly. "Though I think he spent more time at the racing track."

"Right, let's recap. Until you started junior high school in Oita, it was the four of you at home. Then, in the summer of your first year at junior high, your mum left home with your little sister, leaving you in your dad's care. And now you live in Osaka. So . . . when did you leave Oita?"

"Halfway through my second year of senior high school. An Osaka swimming club invited me to move to a school affiliated with Kindai Sports University. I've been living in dormitories ever since."

"So you and your dad lived together for"—Koishi counted on her fingers—"four years, is that right?"

"Yeah. Of course, that meant he had to cook for me. My senior high school in Oita had a cafeteria, but for the three years before that, when I was still at junior high, my dad made me a bento every day."

"And sometimes it was this nori-ben?"

Kyosuke smiled vaguely. "Not sometimes. Always."

"Always?" asked Koishi, her mouth gaping. "You mean . . . every day?"

"I only had myself to blame, really. See, the first time he made it, I made the mistake of telling him I liked it. 'Super yummy,' I think my exact words were. Dad was over the moon. After that he started making it every day." Kyosuke's expression had turned slightly morose.

Koishi sighed. "Got a little carried away, did he?"

"My friends started making fun of me for always eating the exact same thing. I'd hide the inside of my bento with the lid and shovel it down as fast as I could. That's probably why I don't recall much about the flavor. All I do remember is that, well, I *did* like it." Kyosuke said these final words with conviction.

"I've only had nori-ben from bento shops, so I don't know how people make it at home, but . . . was it really just nori and rice? He didn't add a layer of bonito flakes in between?" Koishi drew an illustration in her notepad and showed it to Kyosuke.

"No, you're right—it had three layers. First a layer of rice, then some bonito flakes soaked in soy sauce, and the nori on top. Oh, and a big pickled plum on top." He added these details to Koishi's illustration. "The exact same thing, every day."

"Was there anything distinctive about the flavor? It wasn't particularly sweet or salty or anything?"

"No, nothing like that," replied Kyosuke, staring intently at the drawing. "I think it was pretty ordinary. Though I do remember it being a little on the dry side."

Koishi cocked her head to one side. "Dry? That doesn't sound very tasty. I always thought nori and bonito flakes tasted their best when they still had a bit of moisture."

Kyosuke smiled faintly. "I also seem to remember it being a little . . . sour, sometimes."

"Sour? It hadn't . . . gone bad, had it?" Koishi grinned. "Seriously, though—if it was just rice, bonito flakes, and nori, shouldn't it be fairly easy to re-create?" She traced her finger over the illustration as she spoke.

"That's what I thought too. But when I asked the cook at the cafeteria to make it for me, it just wasn't the same.

Tasted so bland I barely managed to finish it. With my dad's, I'd gobble it right down, and the bento box would be empty before I knew it." A note of passion had crept into Kyosuke's voice.

"Maybe that was just because you were still young," said Koishi, failing to match his enthusiasm. "I mean, it was all you had for lunch, wasn't it? Anyway—weren't you saying you ate it quickly on purpose because you didn't want your friends to see?"

"Well, yeah, but . . ." replied Kyosuke, his enthusiasm waning slightly.

"Was your dad an expert in the kitchen, then?"

"No. In fact, I barely saw him set foot in there until Mum left."

"So this was his one and only signature dish. But . . . what made you want to eat it again all of a sudden?"

"My aunt got in touch. Apparently Dad's condition has gotten worse. She wants me to at least come and visit."

"Why don't you go, then? It'd be your chance to thank him for all those bentos."

Kyosuke frowned. "If he only made them because anything else would have been too much effort, then . . . I don't think I want to see him."

"Really? I still think you should go, personally," Koishi said, shrugging.

"Maybe I will," replied Kyosuke, his jaw clenching

slightly. "But first, I want to remember what that nori-ben tasted like. I think that'll help me understand how he felt about the whole thing."

"Well, we'll do our best—and with a bit of luck, you'll be able to patch things up with your dad. I say we"— Koishi grinned—"but it's my dad who'll do all the investigating."

"Thank you. It means a lot," Kyosuke said, getting to his feet and bowing deeply. His voice had regained its earlier liveliness.

When they returned to the restaurant, Nagare reached for the remote control and switched off the television that sat on a shelf near the entrance.

"Did that all go okay?"

"Oh, it went fine," replied Koishi, "but I think we've got our work cut out for us."

"You always say that. Well, all we can do is try our best. Something tricky, is it?"

"Dad, it's . . . nori-ben."

Kyosuke smiled awkwardly, hunching his shoulders in embarrassment.

"Ah," replied Nagare. "The simplest dishes are always the hardest to get right."

At this, the smile vanished from Kyosuke's lips.

"Don't worry," said Koishi, patting him on the back. "Dad'll work it out."

Kyosuke bowed to them both, then took his leave. As he slid open the door to the restaurant, a tabby cat came rushing over to his feet.

"Hey, you," snapped Nagare, "don't even think about coming in here!"

"We had a tabby back in Oita too," said Kyosuke. "What's its name?"

"Drowsy," replied Koishi. "Sits around all day snoozing, see." She beckoned to the cat, who, warily eyeing Nagare, tiptoed over to her.

"So—when should I come back?" Kyosuke set his bag down from his shoulder and fished out his phone.

"Will two weeks from now be all right?" asked Nagare.

Kyosuke swiped at his phone's screen to check his schedule. "Ah, I have training camp in Kyoto starting next weekend, so that'll be perfect."

"I'll confirm the details by phone," said Koishi, scooping Drowsy up into her arms.

Kyosuke put his phone away, thanked them again, then set off west down the street.

"The Keihan station's the other way, you know!" called Koishi.

Kyosuke stopped, did an about-face, and sighed. "My

sense of direction is atrocious." With an embarrassed grin, he made his way back past them and down the street.

"See you soon," called Nagare from behind him.

Kyosuke stopped again. "Oh. I completely forgot to pay!" He made his way back toward them, sheepishly scratching his head.

"You can pay next time," said Koishi. "Together with the fee for the detective service."

"How much should I, er, bring?" asked Kyosuke, looking helplessly at Koishi.

"Don't worry. It won't be anything excessive," said Nagare.

"Okay. Well, thank you." Kyosuke bowed again, then hurried off down the street.

They watched him go, then returned inside. Drowsy gave a languid *meow*.

"I can't believe an ace athlete like Kyosuke wants us to make him . . . nori-ben," said Koishi, wiping down the table. "Not quite the combination I was expecting!"

"So you're on first-name terms, eh?" said Nagare as he took a seat at the counter and opened up Koishi's notebook. "You two friends or something?"

Koishi's hands froze. "What? Dad, did you seriously not realize?"

"Realize what?" asked Nagare, his expression unchanged as he flicked through the notebook.

"He's a famous swimmer! Going to be in the Olympics and everything. Backstroke, butterfly, freestyle—he can do it all!" Koishi mimed someone swimming front crawl.

"Oh, right," replied Nagare as he retrieved a map from the shelf. "Well, it doesn't really matter who the client is, does it? All we can do is our best."

"Well, yes, but . . ." said Koishi, puffing out her cheeks.

"Oita, eh? That place is a paradise for food lovers. All that delicious mackerel . . . Looks like I'll have to take a little trip."

"Sounds fun! Can I come?"

"Nope. Your job is to look after this place while I'm gone. Don't worry, I'll bring you back a little something. Anyway," he added, glancing toward the altar in the back room, "your mother would get all lonely on her own."

2

The Kindai Sports University training camp was taking place at the Fukakusa school in Kyoto's Fushimi district. A few days after the camp had begun, Kyosuke finally had permission to take the day off. As he boarded the Keihan train, he felt his spirits rise in anticipation.

The train passed Fushimi-Inari station, its building painted the same vermilion color as the famous torii gates

nearby, then a few stations later disappeared under-
ground. When it eventually pulled into Shichijo station,
Kyosuke stepped down onto the platform, a small satchel
slung over his shoulder.

Though this was his second visit, the directionally
challenged Kyosuke soon lost his bearings. With his
heavily creased map in hand, he slowly made his way
through the streets, trying his hardest to remember the
route. Finally, a building he recognized came into view.

Inside, Koishi greeted him with a smile. "Welcome
back!"

"Hello again," replied Kyosuke, before anxiously looking around for Nagare.

"Don't you worry. Dad worked it all out," said Koishi,
setting a glass on the table together with a pitcher of iced
tea. "He's just setting something up in the kitchen, so sit
tight a minute, okay?"

"I could barely sleep last night," said Kyosuke, before
stifling a yawn.

"You're more sensitive than I thought," chuckled Koishi. "Sure you'll be all right at the Olympics?"

"That's different, okay?" replied Kyosuke grumpily.

"Sorry for the wait," said Nagare, poking his head out
from the kitchen. "I, er, thought of something fun we
could try."

"Yeah," said Koishi, "Dad had everything ready—then he had some bright idea and started fiddling around again."

Kyosuke half rose from his chair and tried to peer into the kitchen. "Is . . . everything okay?"

"Oh, I'm sure it's all *completely* under control," replied Koishi, making a wry face.

"Right, then, all ready." Nagare reappeared carrying two bento boxes on a square tray.

Kyosuke, who'd refilled his rice bowl three times at breakfast that morning, winced slightly. "Is that . . . two portions?"

"You don't have to finish both," replied Nagare, setting the lidded bento boxes on the table. "I just want you to compare the taste."

Kyosuke glanced at each of the anodized aluminum boxes in turn. "So they taste different?"

"You'll have to tell *me* that once you've tried them."

Nagare bowed and returned to the kitchen.

Koishi indicated the pitcher of iced tea on the table. "Filled to the brim—but just let me know if you need more." She followed Nagare into the kitchen.

Left on his own, Kyosuke sat up straight, and using one hand for each bento box, he opened them at the same time.

They both looked like nori-ben. A flat layer of nori

NORI-BEN

covered the surface, with joins visible between the individual sheets. He felt a flash of recognition: this was exactly the way his father had made it.

With the long edges of the bento boxes facing him, the
cracks between the sheets of seaweed formed a neat grid
of lines—two horizontal and three vertical—so that each
nori-ben was divided into twelve squares. Staring at the
grid, he vividly recalled how, back then, he had always
finished the bento in precisely twelve mouthfuls.

He began with the left-hand box. Holding it in one
hand, with the long edge still facing him, he dug his
chopsticks around the bottom-left segment and carried it
to his mouth. The nori-ben consisted of three layers: a
layer of rice on the bottom, then bonito flakes, and then
the nori on top. Again, it was just the way his father had
made it.

"Mmm," he murmured. He closed his eyes. He chewed.
Then he moved on to the next segment and devoured
that in the same way. Compared to the one they'd made
him at the cafeteria, this nori-ben was in another league.
It was, in a word, delicious.

In which case . . . what about the other bento? Was it
some sort of failed experiment? Or was it going to be even
tastier than this one?

He inserted his chopsticks into the box on the right.
Just like he'd done with the first one, he dug down into

the bottom-left corner, brought the slab of nori-ben to his mouth, and slowly chewed away. Then he tried the next section, and the one after that, until . . .

As he chewed, a tear fell from the corner of his eye. Then another. And another, and another. Wiping them away with the back of his hand, he reached for the next segment, inserted it into his mouth, and began chewing again. Unable to restrain himself any longer, Kyosuke began quietly sobbing.

The second bento had produced no sudden spike of nostalgia, no overwhelming rush of sadness. To be honest, he had no idea why he was crying.

But the taste was different. He couldn't say why, but the nori-ben his father had made him every day was, without a doubt, the one on the right.

"Did I get it right?"

Nagare had emerged from the kitchen and was standing behind him.

Kyosuke nodded as he rubbed the tears from his eyes. "Yes, this is it."

"Glad to hear it," said Nagare, pouring some iced tea into his glass.

"The one on the left was really tasty, but this one . . ." Kyosuke's eyes began to well with tears again.

"Yes. The one on the right is the bento your dad made

22

for you," said Nagare, looking kindly at him. "Day after day."

"But . . . what's the difference?" asked Kyosuke, sitting up in his chair. "They look identical to me, but when I eat them they're so different."

"There's no big secret here. It's more a question of the lengths your dad went to." Nagare set a folder on the table.

"The lengths he went to . . ." murmured Kyosuke, eyeing the folder.

"The one on the left is tasty enough, isn't it? But your dad had another trick up his sleeve. A way to make the nori-ben not only tasty but also nourishing—while also stopping it from spoiling."

"My dad thought of a thing like that?"

"He was hopeless in the kitchen. One day, partly out of desperation, he tried making you a nori-ben. And you loved it. Afterward, he went to his favorite restaurant and asked them for advice. Told them he wanted to make you the tastiest nori-ben in the country."

"He had a . . . favorite restaurant?"

"Most taxi drivers have a spot they'll always go to for lunch. Somewhere tasty and not too pricey—with decent parking to boot. Your dad drove for a company called Bungo Tours, didn't he? Well, it turns out most of their drivers frequented a casual spot, the Aramiya Diner. That little place, tucked away behind the prefectural office building, was where your father, Kyota Kitano, went for lunch every day. In fact, he was such a regular there that the owner, Mr. Aramiya, remembered him well."

Nagare extracted a photo of the restaurant from the folder and laid it on the table.

Kyosuke gazed down at the photo. "This place?"

"Looks ordinary enough, doesn't it—and yet the fish is exceptional. Oita is full of places like that." Nagare got his phone out and began showing Kyosuke some photos of the food. "I tried the deep-fried horse mackerel—your father's favorite, apparently—and it was far better than any version of it I've ever had in Kyoto."

"You're rambling, Dad," complained Koishi. "Tell him about the nori-ben."

"What's the rush? Anyway, the point is, Mr. Aramiya knows his fish. He comes from a long line of fishermen, and apparently even ran his own sushi place at one point. With someone like that whispering secrets in your father's ear, it's no wonder his nori-ben turned out so delicious."

Nagare picked up the right-hand bento and continued. "Sure, it looks exactly the same. Both on top"—he inserted a pair of chopsticks into the top-right section, which Kyosuke hadn't yet reached—"and when you dig down inside." Koishi and Kyosuke watched as Nagare carefully set the segment on the lid of the bento, revealing the individual layers. "And yet it's not the same."

"Hmm . . . it has the same three layers. Looks identical to me," said Koishi, inspecting it from the side. Kyosuke nodded in agreement.

"The difference is this part in the middle," said Nagare, removing the top layer of nori. "Look carefully. Those aren't bonito flakes, are they?"

"You're right!" exclaimed Koishi, leaning in for a closer look. "Is that . . . fish meat?"

Kyosuke was still gazing blankly, apparently unable to see the difference. Nagare darted into the kitchen, emerging a moment later with a styrofoam box. He held it up in front of the waiting pair, then opened it to reveal a fish.

"Cutlass fish, this is called. See how it looks just like a sword? That's what's in the bento. Grilled, minced, and seasoned with soy sauce and kabosu fruit. Both cutlass fish and kabosu are Oita specialties—and the citric acid in the kabosu stops the dish from spoiling too. If you just use bonito flakes, the flavor can get a little monotonous, but this gives it heaps of depth."

"Cutlass fish, huh?" said Kyosuke, inspecting the filling. "And he chopped it up like this specially?"

"I guess you were in such a hurry to eat it without your friends seeing that you just dug your chopsticks in and shoveled it into your mouth, without ever realizing what you were eating."

"It's true. I don't think I ever properly looked inside."

"With a bit of help from Mr. Aramiya, your dad made you a nori-ben he could be proud of."

Kyosuke smiled through his tears. "I can't believe he managed a thing like this. He always seemed so hopeless."

"Well, it seems that was precisely what endeared him to people. When I asked about him at that restaurant, all the regulars had stories to tell."

"I bet he caused them all sorts of trouble over the years."

"Like I say, there were plenty of stories. But I can tell you this: no one there had a bad word to say about him."

"Well, that's a relief," said Kyosuke. And it was true: he looked as though a heavy weight had been lifted from his shoulders. He was learning about a side to his father he'd never known.

"Apparently one of the other taxi drivers once pointed out to your father that there was no way of knowing you'd actually eaten his bento. The guy thought you might be secretly chucking them in the garbage."

Kyosuke shook his head vigorously.

"Now, your dad was normally the quiet type, but on this occasion, it seems he really flipped. Shouted at the

26

guy, telling him his son would never deceive anyone like that, not in a million years. And he *definitely* wouldn't throw something his father had made him in the garbage."

As Nagare spoke, Kyosuke gazed at the nori-ben.

"Yep," said Koishi, nodding enthusiastically as she tried a bite. "I think that might actually be the best nori-ben in the country."

Kyosuke put the lid back on the bento box. "Thank you both so much. Can I take this home with me?"

"Of course," said Nagare, smiling. "I prepared another one especially for that purpose too. Take them both, if you like."

"I'll get you some ice packs to keep them chilled," said Koishi, running over to the freezer.

"I've written you out the recipe too," said Nagare, inserting the folder into a paper bag, together with the bento boxes. "I'm guessing you're not much of a cook yourself, but as long as you follow the instructions, you should be able to make it just like your father did." He handed Kyosuke the paper bag.

"So, how much do I owe you?" said Kyosuke, reaching for his wallet. "Including for the meal last time, I mean."

"Whatever you feel it was worth. Just pop it in this account." Koishi handed him a slip with the relevant details. "Oh, and factor in a student discount if you like."

Kyosuke carefully folded the piece of paper and inserted it into his wallet. "Thank you."

Koishi grasped his hand. "We'll be rooting for you at the Olympics."

"Thanks," said Kyosuke, his chest swelling slightly as he made his way outside.

Nagare called after him, "I'll bet your dad will be too. It's a big deal, after all!"

Kyosuke reached down to pet Drowsy, who had come rushing over. "Oh, he's probably too busy gambling to even think about me."

"If he made you a nori-ben this good every day, there's no way he's forgotten about you. I'm sure he couldn't even if he tried."

Kyosuke bowed wordlessly in response, then began making his way west down Shomen-dori.

"Wrong way again!" called Koishi from behind.

"Never learn, do I?" said Kyosuke, scratching his head as he turned around and strode past them again, this time heading east.

"Like a fish out of water, isn't he?" chuckled Nagare. "Literally."

Kyosuke suddenly stopped and turned. "I forgot to tell you. I've decided to just swim butterfly from now on."

"Sounds very wise," said Nagare, bowing his head

slightly. As Kyosuke set off down the street again, Drowsy looked in the direction of his departing figure and mewed quietly.

"Dad, there's one thing bothering me," said Koishi when they were back in the restaurant.

"What's that, then?" asked Nagare, glancing at her as he slid the door shut behind them.

"We're not having nori-ben for dinner, are we?"

"*That's* what's bothering you, eh? Well, why not? Nothing wrong with a good old nori-ben and a cup of sake."

"Seriously? Come on," pleaded Koishi, her forehead puckering as she started tidying up.

"I'm joking, obviously," said Nagare as he made his way into the kitchen. "No, it's cutlass fish hot pot tonight. Just as tasty as making it with hamo eel, I reckon."

Koishi's eyes lit up. "Phew. There's the dad I know! That really *will* go well with a cup of sake."

"I picked the fish up from the market in Oita," said Nagare, retrieving the styrofoam box from the fridge. "It's a special brand—Kunisaki Gintachi. I figured we could use it the same way we use hamo eel here in Kyoto, so I really stocked up."

"Fewer bones than hamo too," said Koishi as she carefully wiped the counter down. "It'll be less of a pain to cook."

"Kikuko always loved her hamo," remarked Nagare as he began working away at the fish with his knife.

"Ooh, that gives me an idea!" exclaimed Koishi, poking her head into the kitchen. "What if we made sushi out of it? You know—like with hamo. Mum used to go crazy for that stuff."

"Oh, I already thought of that," said Nagare, stepping up onto the raised tatami floor of the living room. He set a small plate of cutlass fish sushi in front of the altar.

Koishi sat down behind him, joined her hands together, and bowed toward the altar. "I can't wait to try it." She paused. "Once Mum's had her fill, obviously."

Chapter 2

Hamburger Steak

1

Kana Takeda stood fidgeting at the intersection, glaring at the signal as she waited for it to change. For a brief moment, her eyes flicked up toward Kyoto Tower, looming on the other side of Shiokoji-dori, before returning to the signal.

The moment the light turned green, Kana, dressed in a gray pantsuit, began dashing across, beating everyone else to the other side.

"Trust me to come to Kyoto for the last trip of my thirties," she said to herself in an incongruously loud voice. A nearby elderly couple turned and stared.

Kana wheeled her small pink suitcase north up Karasuma-dori with barely a sideways glance. From there, she turned onto Shomen-dori and made a beeline for her destination. When she reached the restaurant, she threw the door open and called out: "Hello!"

Koishi, busy clearing away some dishes, paused and looked up. "Hello?"

"This *is* the Kamogawa Diner, isn't it?" asked Kana, setting her suitcase down in the corner.

"It is," said Koishi brusquely as she loaded plates onto a tray.

Kana unslung her black shoulder bag, set it on the table, then bowed. "There's a dish I'd like you to help me find."

"Oh," said Koishi, her expression relaxing noticeably. "You're here for the detective service, are you?"

"Welcome," said Nagare, emerging from the kitchen and removing his white chef's hat.

"Sorry to barge in like this," said Kana, presenting her business card. "My name is Kana Takeda. I'm here on Akane Daidoji's recommendation."

"Ah," said Nagare. "You must be the drinking buddy Akane was telling me about. She phoned me a couple of weeks ago—mentioned you might drop by." Still gripping her card in one hand, he gestured toward one of the tables. "Please."

"Thank you." Kana gave another quick bow before sitting down.

"Feeling peckish?" asked Nagare as he set her card on the counter. "Can I make you something?"

"I've heard you work wonders in the kitchen. If you're offering, I'd love to try a bite or two."

"Akane's been spreading rumors about me, has she? I can't promise anything special, but I can certainly whip up a few seasonal dishes. Is there anything you don't like?"

"Oh, I'll eat anything you put in front of me."

"Right, then. Just give me a moment." Nagare replaced his hat and hurried back into the kitchen.

"*Food writer* . . ." said Koishi, eyeing the business card on the counter. "So you write for magazines and things?"

"Yes, magazines and newspapers," Kana said, smiling. "I've done a bit of television work recently too."

"Wow, lucky you. Eating like royalty—and making a living from it to boot. What a life!"

"It isn't always that rosy." Kana shrugged. "And these days work's drying up."

Koishi set a Karatsu-ware cup in front of Kana and filled it with tea. "So you work with Akane, then?"

Kana shrugged again. It appeared to be a habit of hers. "Actually, we only partnered on something the one time, but we just sort of hit it off. Maybe it's something to do with both being single mothers. We go out drinking a couple of times a month."

"So you enjoy a tipple, then? What can I get you?"

"I'd like to see the food before I decide, if you don't mind."

"I had a feeling you'd say that," said Nagare, returning

from the kitchen and laying an indigo-dyed cloth over the table.

Kana gave him a cheeky look. "Am I that easy to read?"

"Akane tells me you're a wine drinker. As you've probably guessed from the looks of this place, we don't have anything too fancy—but I'll fish you out one of my favorites."

Nagare made his way back to the kitchen.

Koishi began smoothing out the wrinkles in the table-cloth. "I made this with my mum when we went to Tokushima. At an indigo-dyeing workshop."

"It's a lovely color." A wistful look crossed Kana's face. "I wish I'd been on trips like that with *my* mother."

"Is she a career woman like you, then?"

"Not exactly. She helps my dad run his business."

"What sort of business is that, then?"

"A little restaurant. Up north in Hirosaki."

"Like this place, you mean?"

"Oh, it couldn't hold a candle to anywhere in Kyoto," said Kana dryly. "It's just one of those casual places that does a bit of everything—ramen, curry, you name it."

"Sounds just like us," Koishi said, grinning.

Nagare returned from the kitchen carrying a large vine-woven basket layered with light green paper, in which he'd arranged various small bowls and plates of food.

"Thought I might as well give you the full picnic experience, seeing as spring's finally here."

"Oh my," said Kana. "Mind if I take a photo?" She was already reaching for the digital camera in her bag.

"I'm not sure any of this is worth it, to be honest. But go ahead."

He had barely finished speaking when she began snapping away with the camera in her left hand.

"Once a journalist, always a journalist, eh?" said Koishi with a wry grin.

"The moment I see anything delicious . . ." Kana carried on taking photos, rapidly adjusting her angle and zoom after each shot.

"All done?" asked Nagare when the shutter finally stopped clicking.

"Yes. Sorry about that," said Kana, hastily putting the camera back in her bag.

"I've prepared you a selection of spring fare. Starting from the top left—"

"Wait a minute," said Kana. She scrabbled around in her bag, then produced a pen-shaped voice recorder, which she activated and set on the table. "Okay, ready." She glanced up to see Nagare making a pained smile.

"Right," he continued. "In the top left you have simmered Nagaoka bamboo shoots and wakame seaweed from Izumo, served in a Karatsu-ware bowl. Next to that, on the long Oribe dish, is grilled masu salmon seasoned with pepper tree leaves. The square Kutani bowl is dashi-simmered egg scrambled with green peas. The next row down is a series of five small Imari plates. Starting on the left: white miso clam gratin; salad of finely chopped cockles and Kujo green onion; tilefish sashimi with a ponzu, miso, and pepper-tree-leaf dressing; slow-cooked Tamba chicken in a salt koji marinade. At the end, on the right, is pickled sweetfish sushi, served whole. The round dish at the bottom is a selection of wild vegetables: butterbur buds, devil's-walking-stick, ostrich fern, momiji-gasa, bracken shoots, and smilax. Normally those would be served as tempura, but I've gone for something a little different and deep-fried them Western-style instead. Sprinkle them with matcha salt if you like, or they go very nicely with this green peppercorn–infused Worcestershire sauce." Nagare produced a bottle of white wine. "Now, will something like this do?"

"Hang on a moment," said Kana, reaching for her digital camera again.

"My friend in Tamba makes this," continued Nagare. "Hundred percent Chardonnay grapes, fermented in small French casks, apparently. Has an elegant, tart flavor—perfect for spring, I'd say." He uncorked the bottle and filled Kana's glass.

"Ah," said Kana, holding the cork to her nose. "That's a wonderful bouquet." Then, gripping the stem of her glass with three fingers, she took a sip.

Her eyes lit up. "That's quite something!" she exclaimed, reaching for the bottle and inspecting it.

"Glad you like it. I don't think it needs serving any colder than that, or I'd have brought out a wine bucket. Drink as much as you'd like."

With that, Nagare returned to the kitchen, followed by Koishi.

The silence that descended over the restaurant was broken only by the sound of the voice recorder being switched off. Kana surveyed the contents of the basket once more.

"Hmm, let's start with the deep-fried vegetables," she said to herself, sprinkling some of the matcha salt over the butterbur buds before taking a bite. After an initial satisfying crunch, she felt an explosion of bitterness in her mouth, followed by a faint but lingering sweetness.

"Interesting," she murmured, getting out her notebook. With her pen in her left hand, she began scribbling away.

Next, gripping her chopsticks with her right hand, she reached for one of the deep-fried bracken shoots and, after a moment's hesitation, dipped it in the small dish of Worcestershire sauce before inserting it into her mouth.

"Ah." She nodded. "Yes, the sauce works very well too." She carried on making notes with her left hand.

Once she had made her way through the deep-fried vegetables, her eyes darted toward the top row of dishes.

She crunched on one of the bamboo shoots. "These always taste that little bit more special in Kyoto." She filled a few more lines of her notebook.

After another sip of wine, she moved on to the masu salmon and clam gratin, murmuring to herself after each mouthful. This time, she set the chopsticks down and picked up her pen with her right hand. Her left hand was occupied; it was firmly gripping the wineglass.

Finally, as she finished off the tilefish sashimi, she murmured to herself, "I think this is our winner," and drew three stars next to it in her notebook.

"How are you getting on?" asked Nagare. He had emerged from the kitchen with a silver tray in his hand, and now cast an eye over the depleted contents of the basket.

"This is remarkable," replied Kana, smiling as she set down the wineglass in order to underline something with her pen. "I've eaten at my fair share of Kyoto restaurants, but this is easily in the top three."

"I'm honored," said Nagare, his expression unchanged. "Though I don't know if you can really call this Kyoto cuisine. They're just nibbles to go with your wine, really."

"You're being modest again," said Kana, jabbing him gently in the belly with an elbow. "This is Michelin star–worthy stuff!"

"By the way," said Nagare, changing the topic, "I'm impressed you can use both hands like that."

"Yes, well . . ." Kana shrugged. "I've too many things to do at once."

"How about some rice to finish off? Today it's cooked with butterbur and sakura shrimp."

"Wonderful. But . . . could I have another glass of wine first?"

"Of course. I'll bring you the rice a little later, together with today's soup." Tucking his silver tray under one arm, Nagare returned to the kitchen.

As she poured herself the wine, Kana's gaze scanned the middle row of the basket. She reached for the small square Kutani bowl and held it under her nose.

There was something vaguely nostalgic about the distinctive smell of the green peas. She picked up the small spoon that had been positioned by the bowl, then scooped up one of the large, egg-covered peas and popped it into her mouth.

Her gaze returned to the basket, this time settling on the small sweetfish that had been pickled and served whole as sushi. Kana reached for her digital camera again, this time getting as close to the dish as possible.

Her lens was almost touching the fish. On the camera's screen, its skin glistened irresistibly.

All of a sudden, Kana remembered when, as a young girl, her father had taken her fishing in the neighboring prefecture.

After dangling her line in the water for what seemed like forever, she had finally landed a sweetfish. Its scales had shimmered in the summer sun as it flipped from side to side, almost as if it were pleading for its life. But when she'd told her father that if they were just here to enjoy catching it, they might as well throw it back in the river, he had scolded her sharply.

"Catching a fish is the same as killing it. It's just like with meat, or even vegetables: when you eat them, you're taking life. Why else do you think we always give thanks before our meals? You catch a fish, Kana, you'd better well eat it."

She had barely started primary school at the time, and her dislike for this lecturing tone must have shown on her face. A moment later, her father had slapped her.

It wasn't an incident that had scarred her deeply, but she still remembered it from time to time. Whenever it did, she felt an unsettling bitterness rising up from the pit of her stomach.

Somehow, it felt as though all the tension between her and her father could be traced back to that one moment.

She focused her lens on the sweetfish sushi, feeling the memories wash through her.

When she had almost finished the contents of the basket, Nagare appeared with a small clay pot.

"Young sakura shrimp from the sea, and butterbur shoots from the mountains—all cooked together with the rice." Nagare dished some of the rice from the pot into a small rice bowl. "Spring's the time of new life, after all. It's lightly seasoned, so you can enjoy it as it is—or put a dollop of this butterbur miso on top and then pour tea over it if you'd prefer it chazuke-style. I'll just fetch the soup." He set off for the kitchen again.

The time of new life, thought Kana, digesting what Nagare had just said. Why had those words triggered another rush of memories? Was it because Nagare was about her father's age, or because he also worked with food for a living? With these thoughts swirling in her mind, Kana tried a mouthful of the rice.

"Incredible."

Without even remembering to take a photo, she began shoveling the rice into her mouth.

In next to no time, her bowl was empty. Just as she began refilling it from the pot, Nagare appeared at her side with an oblong tray on which he'd positioned a small soup bowl.

"How's that, then?"

Kana looked up with a smile as she served herself the rice. "Even tastier than I was expecting."

"Glad to hear it. The sakura shrimp fishing season has just started in Yui, so that's the first catch you're eating. If you believe what they say, that means you'll live a long and healthy life."

Nagare removed the lid from the bowl, releasing a cloud of steam. Kana leaned over, closed her eyes, and took a deep sniff of the clear broth.

"It smells wonderful!"

"The only solid ingredient is diced tofu. Plus a garnish of pepper tree leaves."

"Just tofu? But this aroma—it's so complex."

"The stock is from quick-grilled sweetfish bones. I had plenty of them left over from all that sushi."

"So that's what I'm picking up," replied Kana, sniffing the steam again. "Who'd have thought those tiny little bones could add so much flavor?"

"Did you know that one way of writing 'sweetfish' is to use the characters for 'year' and 'fish'? The poor things only live for a year, see. All the more reason to make sure we eat every last bit of them."

Again, Nagare's words seemed to make a deep impression, and the normally talkative Kana fell abruptly silent.

"Well, when you're finished, I'll show you to the office

at the back." Nagare retrieved his tray and disappeared into the kitchen once more.

Kana raised the bowl of broth to her lips. The tofu, diced into five-millimeter cubes, slipped smoothly down her throat, while the fragrance of the sweetfish and pepper tree leaves filled her nostrils. She let out a deep, satisfied sigh. All this talk about the preciousness of life had very little to do with actually enjoying your meal, she thought to herself.

She had soon drained the entire bowl of broth, but the clay pot was still one-third full of rice. Kana's cheeks had flushed, probably because of how much she'd had to drink.

"Ah," she said, remembering Nagare's suggestion. "Almost forgot to try it chazuke-style." Hastily, she transferred the remaining rice to her bowl, spooned over some of the butterbur miso, then reached for the teapot and poured hot green tea over the lot.

She picked up her chopsticks and began quietly slurping away at the chazuke rice. Without her expression changing in the slightest, she devoured the entire bowl, right down to the last grain of rice. Just as she was gently setting her chopsticks down, Nagare reappeared.

"Right, then, shall I show you to the office?"

"Please," replied Kana, almost jumping to her feet.

Nagare opened the door adjoining one end of the counter and led Kana down a corridor.

"That really was a wonderful meal," said Kana from behind.

"Yoroshu, o-agari," said Nagare, turning with a smile.

"Sorry?"

"Yoroshu, o-agari," repeated Nagare, this time stopping as he turned around. "It's a Kyoto expression. We say it when someone thanks you for a meal. Means something like, 'Thanks for eating it.' You won't usually hear it in restaurants, mind."

"Ah. That makes sense."

"You have kids, don't you? What do *you* say when they thank you for dinner?"

"'Sorry it wasn't much.'"

"I don't mean to be rude," said Nagare with a vague smile, "but just what sort of grub are you serving them?"

Kana turned red. "Oh, it's just a turn of phrase, I think."

"Ah. My apologies." Nagare bowed before setting off again. Kana shrugged and followed him to the end of the corridor, where he knocked on the door.

"Please," called Koishi from inside, "come on in!"

Nagare saw Kana into the room, then returned to the restaurant.

"Do you think you could fill this out for me?" Koishi handed a clipboard and pen to Kana, who sat down on the sofa opposite her. With the pen in her left hand, Kana began scribbling away.

"You're left-handed, then?"

Kana smiled as she returned the clipboard. "Actually, my father forced me to use my right hand as a child. So now I can use both."

"I see," said Koishi, scanning the form. "Thirty-nine, eh? How are you feeling about the big four-zero?"

"To be honest, I can't believe it's come so soon."

"Well, I should probably start bracing myself too. So, Kana Takeda, what's the dish you'd like us to re-create?" As she spoke, Koishi set her phone on the table and pressed something on its screen. "By the way, I couldn't help noticing how you recorded your chat with Dad just now. Thought I'd copy you! I'm so ditzy these days— always forgetting the most important details. This way, it doesn't matter if I miss something. Anyway, go ahead. What's the dish?"

"A hamburger steak."

"Ah." Koishi opened her notebook. "Japanese-style, with just the steak? Not a full-on hamburger?"

"That's right. But not the fancy type you get at proper restaurants. Something a bit more basic and homemade—the kind you might find at a cheap diner. Not that I'd include this place in that category, mind. The food's far too delicious for that!"

"No need to flatter us," said Koishi, flashing a slightly forced smile before she went on. "So, when and where did you eat this hamburger steak?"

"Well, I think my father made it."

"You *think*?"

"Actually, I wasn't even the one who ate it. I suppose I should explain." Kana sat up and cleared her throat.

"Bit of a tangled tale, is it?" asked Koishi, leaning forward and readying her pen.

"I have a six-year-old son. Yusuke. He's the one who ate it."

"And your father made it?"

"I can't think who else could have."

"Hmm," said Koishi, rolling her head from side to side in confusion. "Not sure I follow."

"When Yusuke finished nursery school, they made him a special album. There was a section where he had to write his favorite food, and he wrote: 'hamburger steak.' But I've never made him one, and we've never eaten anything like that in a restaurant. The only thing I can think of is the year before last, when I went back to Hirosaki to tell my father that it was just me and Yusuke at home now. I went out during the day, and it seems my father made Yusuke something to eat while I was gone." Kana frowned. "That's the only time he could have had a hamburger steak."

"But it's always a popular dish with kids, isn't it?" replied Koishi. "Are you sure he didn't have it for lunch at nursery school or something?"

"They don't provide lunch at his nursery. Everyone brings their own bento box."

"And you never put a hamburger steak in his bento?"

"No. You have to realize that my husband was very particular when it came to food. He refused to eat meat or fish that had been processed in any way. Minced beef, tsukune meatballs—he couldn't stand that kind of thing, and I felt similarly, so Yusuke never had anything like that."

"I feel sorry for him," said Koishi, unable to stop herself. "Even the frozen ones can be pretty tasty, you know."

Kana's expression grew severe. "Well, *I* feel sorry for kids who are forced to eat meals stuffed with additives, preservatives, and MSG."

"But you wouldn't have to use anything ready-made," said Koishi, determined to make her point. "You could grind the beef yourself and make it at home."

"What'd be the point?" replied Kana, standing her

ground. "I'd just be ruining a perfectly good cut of beef. I don't see why anyone would opt for a substitute over the real thing."

"It's not a *substitute*!" exclaimed Koishi in a shrill voice.

An awkward silence ensued. It was Koishi who eventually broke it. "Sorry. Got a little carried away there."

"No, no," said Kana, bowing her head slightly. "I was rather rude myself."

"Well, getting back to the matter at hand, if it *was* your father who made it, can't you just ask him for the recipe?"

"We're not on very good terms, unfortunately," said Kana, her lips tightening. "I haven't even been back to Hirosaki this year, or last. I can't just suddenly call him up and ask him for a hamburger recipe! And the last thing I want to do is tell him it's Yusuke's favorite."

"Well, I don't know what caused this rift between you, but you're father and daughter, aren't you? I can't help feeling it'd be easier just to go ahead and ask him." Koishi looked pleadingly up at Kana, but she was staring glumly off to one side. "All right, don't worry. I'll get Dad on the case. He can visit your father's restaurant and try this hamburger steak. That'll tell him everything he needs to know."

"No, that won't be enough," said Kana, turning to face her before continuing. "See, I have no way of knowing whether the hamburger steak he served Yusuke was the same one he normally serves at the restaurant. Your father will need to ask about that too. But please," she added suddenly, "I really don't want my father to know it was me who put you up to this."

Koishi looked troubled. "But how's Dad supposed to—"

"Wait, I have an idea," said Kana. "He could pretend to be a journalist. We get all sorts of them at the restaurant, and my father never turns them down. Especially if you told him it was for *Gourmet Monthly*—he'd be delighted. If we can just get Akane in on it, it'll be perfect!" A mischievous grin had spread across Kana's face.

"Very clever. Not sure Dad'll be up for it, though. He hates deceiving people. I guess we'll have to leave the exact method up to him. Anyway, what's the restaurant called?" Koishi readied her pen once more.

"The Takeda Diner. The place has been around for almost a century." Kana reached into her bag, produced a photograph of the restaurant, and laid it on the table.

"Ooh, all buried in the snow—very atmospheric. Is this an old photo, then?"

"No, it's from three years ago. I think the only reason

the place gets so much media attention is because of how ancient it is."

"I didn't know restaurants like this still existed," said Koishi, picking up the photo and gazing at it. "A century old, did you say? Wow. Maybe I should go there myself."

Kana shrugged. "It might look good in photos, but you'd be disappointed."

"By the way," said Koishi as she returned the photo, "why the sudden urge to try this particular dish?"

"It's for Yusuke, really. See, I want him to have a chance to compare two dishes. The dish *I* think is tastiest, and his so-called favorite—that hamburger steak." Kana tucked the photo into a notepad, which she returned to her bag.

"What's this dish of yours, then?"

"In all my years of writing about food, the tastiest thing I've ever eaten was a tournedos Rossini from a steakhouse in Shirokane. A pan-fried filet of Yamagata beef, topped with seared slices of foie gras and truffle. Simple enough, but the flavors were out of this world. I've never been more tempted to use the word *perfection*."

Koishi gave her a dubious look. "You know, I'm not sure it makes much sense to compare a hamburger steak with something that fancy."

"Once Yusuke has had another chance to try it, I'm

going to take him to that steakhouse for a tournedos Rossini. Teach him what real cooking tastes like!"

Koishi sighed deeply. "Right. Now I get it."

"I want Yusuke to grow up to become a globally minded young man. People might make fun of him for not having a father, but I want him to have the very best in life. I don't just mean nice clothes and so on—I'm going to make him into a man of discernment. Which is why I can't have him going around saying his favorite dish is a hamburger steak from some shabby old restaurant in the countryside!"

Koishi placed a hand on her chest. She had gone red in the face but, with a visible effort, swallowed the words that were on the tip of her tongue.

"Right, then. I'll get Dad on the case." She closed her notebook and pressed her phone to end the recording.

"Thank you." Kana bowed slightly and swiftly rose to her feet.

"How was that, then?" asked Nagare, folding away his newspaper and turning to Koishi as the pair reentered the restaurant.

"Oh, we had a very good chat," said Kana, before bowing and adding, "I'm counting on you."

"I'll give it my best shot," replied Nagare. He turned back to Koishi. "Did you make arrangements for next time?"

Koishi turned casually to Kana. "Will two weeks be okay?"

"Certainly," said Kana, shouldering her bag and pulling out the handle of her suitcase. "I assume you'll send it by refrigerated shipping—together with the recipe? I'll pay the postage, of course."

"Send it?" said Koishi, giving her a baffled look. "Oh no, that's not how we do things. Anyway, we'll need to talk you through the meal."

"But Yusuke starts primary school in two weeks," Kana said, pouting. "I'll be rushed off my feet getting him ready!"

"I'm sure you will be," said Nagare, smiling gently at her. "But I can't serve you a meal by post, I'm afraid. I'd really appreciate it if you could come in person."

"Right. Well, I'll see what I can do." With a shrug, Kana slid open the door of the restaurant and stepped outside.

"Stopping off somewhere?" asked Nagare, glancing at her large suitcase as he followed her out.

Kana shrugged again. "I thought I'd check out a few restaurants that have just opened in town. For our Kyoto issue in the autumn."

"Ah. Staying overnight, then?"

"Yes. A new hotel on the banks of the Kamogawa."

"Will Yusuke be all right on his own?" asked Koishi, reaching down to pick up Drowsy, who had sprawled himself at her feet.

"He's with the sitter tonight," said Kana. With a final bow, she turned and made her way east along Shomen-dori.

"Take care!" called Nagare. When she had disappeared from view, he turned and glared at Drowsy.

"All right, Dad, no need for the evil eye," protested Koishi. "I won't let him in. And you know better than to try, don't you, Drowsy? Go on, off you trot!" She set the cat back down and gave him a little wave.

Back inside, Nagare seated himself at one of the tables. "Right, then, what's the dish?"

"Hamburger steak," replied Koishi flatly.

"Okay. From a particular restaurant?"

"You could say that." Koishi sat down opposite Nagare and opened up her notebook on the table.

"You've hardly written anything." Nagare frowned, flicking through the pages. "What am I supposed to do with this?"

"Don't worry—I've got a secret weapon." Koishi set her phone on the table and tapped away at the screen until the recording started to play.

"Always looking for new ways to slack off, aren't you?" said Nagare, reluctantly leaning in to listen.

"That lady was a real pain, Dad. I don't know what Akane sees in her."

"Hey, enough of that," said Nagare forcefully, still hovering over the phone. "Our job is to find the dish our client asks for. There's nothing else to it."

"Just wait for the bit at the end," said Koishi, opening her notebook to the relevant page. "She wants you to lie to her father!"

"Lie to him?"

"I'll fast-forward it so you can hear for yourself. I just know you'll hate it." Koishi swiped at her phone screen, then shrugged as if in imitation of Kana. After listening to the section in question, Nagare turned to Koishi with a smile.

"Oh, I don't know. Sounds quite fun to me. Just imagine—your old man, pretending to be a food writer!"

"But, Dad . . . You'd be deceiving him."

"You know Shotaro Ikenami, the writer? I read somewhere that he used to do something similar when the mood took him. He'd be staying in a hotel somewhere and start telling people he was a medicine salesman from Toyama or something, just for kicks. Apparently he used to call it 'going undercover.'"

"Well, I guess it's not exactly a crime. But still . . ."

"I'll head to Hirosaki first thing tomorrow."

"Better bring me back something tasty!" said Koishi, slapping him on the shoulder. Nagare simply frowned in response.

2

Cherry blossom season was in full swing, and Kyoto was heaving with visitors. Weaving through the crowds, a small pink shoulder bag at her side, Kana soon found herself standing outside the Kamogawa Diner. Drowsy glanced up at her from his spot by the door, then yawned lazily.

"Hello," she called, sliding the door open and stepping inside.

"Hello again! Lovely day, isn't it," replied Koishi, glancing up at the spring sky before closing the door again.

Nagare appeared from the kitchen and removed his hat. "Good to see you again."

Kana unshouldered her bag and bowed slightly. "I'm looking forward to the meal."

"I know you must be very busy, but I hope you'll try it yourself before you go—fresh from the kitchen. I've prepared a portion to take home with you too."

"Well, all right, then," said Kana, glancing at her watch as she pulled out one of the folding chairs.

"It'll just be a moment." Nagare hurried back into the kitchen.

"What'd you like to drink?" asked Koishi as she wiped the table down.

"I can't stay long," replied Kana curtly as she began swiping away at her phone. "I'll stick with tea today."

Koishi filled a teapot with hot water from a large thermos. A hush fell over the restaurant, only to be broken by a series of loud, evenly spaced thumps from the kitchen, reminiscent of the sound of sticky rice being pounded into mochi. This was followed by a high-pitched hissing and crackling like the spatter of sparks from a flame. Before long, a tempting aroma was drifting over to Kana's table. She raised her eyes from her phone screen as her nose began to twitch.

"It smells fantastic."

"I thought so too at first," said Koishi, giving a little half smile as she filled a Kiyomizu teacup for Kana. "But try smelling it every day for two weeks."

Kana put her phone away in her bag and bowed her head slightly. "Sorry. I did ask rather a lot of you two."

"Not at all. I mean, it's our job. Dad's a real perfectionist—he cooks everything hundreds of times until he's happy with the result. And I'm the designated taste-tester, which explains this. . . ." Koishi patted her slightly round belly through her black apron.

"Ready in there, Koishi?" called Nagare through the curtain separating the kitchen from the restaurant.

Koishi positioned a yellow place mat in front of Kana, together with a small fork and a similarly diminutive pair of chopsticks. "Yep—we're all set!"

"A Mickey Mouse fork, and Donald Duck chopsticks," said Kana. "Getting the Happy Meal, am I?"

Koishi chuckled. "Dad insisted. Said it was all part of the culinary experience."

Just then, Nagare arrived carrying a silver tray. On it, sitting on a round white Western-style plate, was the hamburger steak.

"This, I believe, is the dish Yusuke was so keen on," said Nagare as he set the plate on the mat. "Please, tuck in while it's hot."

"I'll leave the teapot here, but just let me know if you need a refill." With a smile, Koishi followed Nagare back into the kitchen.

Kana got her digital camera from her bag and snapped a few photos.

The hamburger steak in front of her looked just like any other. It was smeared with a red sauce that looked more like simmered-down ketchup than the demi-glace sauce that usually came with hamburger steaks served this way. On top of that was a fried egg, its yolk still runny, and on the side were some french fries, glazed carrots, and buttered corn. This too was all par for the course. To top it off, there was even a small side portion of tomato spaghetti—the kind kids went wild for.

Kana let out a deep sigh before, somewhat reluctantly, breaking off a bite-size piece of the steak with her chopsticks and raising it to her lips.

She had chewed for only a moment when she stopped.

"Wait," she said loudly. "What's *in* this?"

Swapping her chopsticks for the fork, she hacked off a larger part of the burger, rolled it around in the red sauce, and stuffed it into her mouth.

As she slowly chewed, she gazed up at the ceiling and, after a moment, closed her eyes.

Kana's ears suddenly filled with the burble of conversation, like the wind racing down a valley. Her father's low, gravelly voice after a few too many drinks; her mother's high-pitched giggle; her little brother protesting loudly about something. There they all were, happily sharing a meal around the small, low dining table in the living room that was only a couple of tatami mats wide. *That was what it tasted like.* And yet Kana was sure it had been soba for dinner that evening. . . .

With a puzzled expression, she pierced the yolk of the

egg and smeared it all over another piece of the steak before slipping it into her mouth. Then she tried the carrots, the french fries, the corn. One by one, she speared them with her fork and ferried them to her lips.

As she ate, she noticed the tension dissipating from her shoulders. Not just her shoulders, in fact—her fingertips, the crown of her head, her knees, even her heels. It was as though she were floating gently up into the air.

"Well, do you like it?"

Nagare had appeared at her side with a Mashiko-ware earthen teapot.

"You know, I've tried all sorts of hamburger steaks, at all sorts of restaurants, but I've never had anything like this. And yet it tastes somehow . . ." Kana looked up and let out a deep sigh.

Nagare smiled gently at her. "Familiar?"

"Yes! But . . . why?" She frowned. An almost accusing tone had crept into her voice. "I don't remember ever having hamburger steak as a child."

"Taste is a peculiar thing," began Nagare, reaching for a Karatsu-ware teacup and filling it with green tea. "The taste of home, for example. It's different for everyone—and I don't just mean the food. Every family has its own flavor too. The feeling of safety you get from being together, the way you look out for each other—all that combines to create a unique sensation. When you were little, I bet you sat there at the dining table just like this, with your own special plate and cutlery."

Though not entirely convinced by Nagare's words, Kana decided to remain silent for now.

"This plate, chopsticks, and fork are the ones your father actually gives children who come to his restaurant," said Koishi. "Dad went and borrowed them. Claimed he wanted to take photos of them for *Gourmet Monthly*." She winked at Kana.

"I was breaking out in a cold sweat, let me tell you," continued Nagare. "Akane had phoned him in advance for me, so he fell for it hook, line, and sinker. Felt awful tricking him like that, you know."

"So you didn't tell him I sent you, then?" said Kana, smiling with evident relief.

"I didn't mention your name, no. But your father did."

Kana's expression froze. "What?"

"Well, he thought I edited a food magazine, so he must have planned it in advance. Suddenly turns to me and says: 'Do you know Kana Takeda, by any chance?'" Chuckling to himself, Nagare handed her a photo of her father, Yoshio Takeda.

"Ah. He hasn't changed at all."

"I played dumb—told him I wasn't sure. Well, he didn't like that. Told me any food journalist worth their salt would know the name. Really flew off the handle, he did!"

"Must be proud of his daughter," said Koishi, before adding with a pout, "Not like some other dads I know."

"I saw that he had a hamburger steak prix fixe on the menu, so I asked him how he made it." Nagare retrieved the recipe from a file and showed it to her.

"But was it the one Yusuke ate, I wonder?" asked Kana with a worried expression.

"I was asking myself the same question as I ate it. So I tried sounding him out. I said, 'Do you have any grand-children? I bet they'd love this.' He leaned over with this proud look on his face and said, 'It was a big hit with my grandson. He wouldn't stop saying how tasty it was. Even asked for seconds!' So yes—I think we can be pretty sure it's the one Yusuke ate."

Kana scanned the recipe, then gave him a puzzled look. "Soybean flour?"

"Yes. Apparently he uses it to bind the hamburger. You know, just like in Tsugaru soba—your hometown's pride and joy." Nagare produced a leaflet about the soft soba noodles that were a Hirosaki specialty.

Now that she knew why the hamburger steak tasted so familiar, Kana wrinkled her nose in embarrassment. Tsugaru soba was the most popular dish at the Takeda Diner—and the subject of most of the articles that were written about it. Before moving to Tokyo, she'd eaten it almost every day, but she remembered it tasting rather bland compared to the higher-grade, one hundred percent buckwheat soba you could get in the capital. It seemed ridiculous to have felt so nostalgic for an ingredient that was, to her, synonymous with poverty.

"It's very . . . easy on the palate, I'll give you that," she said, skimming through the recipe before returning it to the file. "But compared to a steak . . ."

Koishi had turned red. "Why on earth would you want to *compare* them?"

Kana frowned in response. "As I told you last time, I want Yusuke to be a discerning young man. I want him to develop a taste for the finer things in life—and that includes food."

"But that's just your opinion as his parent!" exclaimed Koishi, staring back at her. "What about what he actually wants?"

"I understand what you're saying. But it's my duty as his mother to raise him properly," said Kana, nodding repeatedly as if trying to convince herself.

"And you're sure that isn't just your ego talking?"

"Koishi!" barked Nagare, his expression stern.

Pouting with frustration, Koishi glanced sideways to see that Kana was simply staring off into space. The three of them had come to a deadlock, and an uncomfortable silence descended.

"I heard about your husband," said Nagare eventually.

Koishi turned away, a surprised look on her face. Kana looked similarly taken aback. After a short pause, she gave a brief nod.

"If I hadn't sent him to the shops that day, he'd still be with us," she said, biting her lip.

Caught up in her work, Kana had asked her husband to do the shopping. On the way, he'd been hit by a truck. It was an incident that had marked her for life.

"I had no idea," said Koishi, her expression darkening.

"Your father told me what happened," said Nagare quietly. "I suppose he opened up because he thought I worked in the same industry as you. He and your mother took turns filling me in."

Kana was still biting her lip, her eyes fixated on the floor.

"It's tough enough being a mother, but you've had to be a father too. It's been hard work, I'll bet. I imagine that's why you want Yusuke to have only the best things in life?"

Kana gave a barely perceptible nod.

"As his only parent, you've given it your all," said Nagare, gently laying his hands on Kana's shoulders. "But maybe it's time to let your foot off the pedal slightly. From now on, why don't you try going easy on him sometimes? I'm sure that's what your husband would have wanted too."

At first Kana's shoulders remained motionless. Then they began to tremble ever so slightly. Soon they were shaking uncontrollably.

"I didn't want having only one parent to ever feel like a burden," she said, pursing her lips firmly. "That's why I raised him this way."

The restaurant fell silent again. From time to time, a burst of noise would come from outside, before fading like a receding tide.

"Sure, it might not be able to compete with a premium cut of beef in terms of pure flavor," said Nagare. "But the hamburger steak is seasoned with a special ingredient: hard work. You have to mix the minced meat with the other ingredients, then work it into a patty with your hands. That's how the love gets in. It's just like making someone a rice ball: you can't help but think affectionately about the person you're making it for. Yusuke might just be a kid, but I'm guessing that when he ate that hamburger steak at his grandfather's restaurant, it tasted like—well, love."

"I tried a few of them myself," said Koishi, gesturing at the now-empty plate, which was decorated with superhero characters. "They are . . . soothing, somehow, aren't they?" She wiped the corner of her eye with her little finger.

Nagare smiled at Kana. "You know, kids are happy eating anything, as long as they can tell it was made with love."

"I suppose you're right," said Kana, bowing her head. The skin around her eyes was smudged with mascara.

"Want me to fix your makeup?" asked Koishi.

"Don't worry," Kana said, smiling warmly. "I'll do it in the bathroom at the station."

"Well, here's the portion for Yusuke—together with the recipe," said Koishi, handing her a paper bag.

"That reminds me. I completely forgot to pay last time." Kana reached into her pink bag and retrieved a long wallet of the same color. "How much do I owe you in total?"

"Oh, just pay what you think it was worth. Here are our details." Koishi slipped a sheet of paper inside a white envelope and handed it to her.

"All right, then," replied Kana, inserting the envelope into her wallet.

Nagare followed her out of the restaurant. "Well, good luck with everything."

"Thanks for all your help." As she bowed, Drowsy came bouncing over.

"Hey," said Nagare, glaring at him, "you'll get her clothes dirty."

"Oh, I don't mind," said Kana, before squatting down to pet the cat.

"Spring really is here, isn't it?" said Koishi, looking up at the blue sky.

Kana followed her gaze. "I'll cook that hamburger as a bento for Yusuke. We can have a picnic under the cherry blossoms."

"Very good," murmured Nagare.

Kana made to leave, then turned. "I meant to ask. That sauce . . . it had an unusual flavor."

"Worcestershire sauce and ketchup, reduced in the pan. Plus a dash of kenoshiru soup."

"Kenoshiru soup, eh . . ." Kana gazed off into space for a moment, then began slowly making her way down the street.

"He's a kind man, your father," called Nagare from behind.

"Give Yusuke our regards," called Koishi.

Kana turned, raised a hand, and waved goodbye.

Back in the restaurant, Nagare sat at the counter and opened up his newspaper.

"Fancy a nighttime picnic under the cherries? We could cook ourselves the rest of the hamburger meat and take it as a bento."

"Sounds like a plan," replied Koishi. "We'll have to take something nice to drink too."

"Says here that the blossoms are looking spectacular at the Imperial Palace," said Nagare, eyeing the cherry blossom forecast in the newspaper.

"Dad, what was that soup you mentioned just now?" asked Koishi as she wiped the table down. "Kenoshiru, did you say?"

"Chopped vegetables—daikon, carrot, and so on—deep-fried tofu, and konnyaku, simmered in kombu stock. Apparently the trick is to mix in something called jinda—mashed soybeans, basically—right at the end."

"Why did you say that made her father a kind man?" asked Koishi as she made her way into the living room.

"See, the snow's so deep in winter up there that they can't pick the traditional seven herbs of spring," replied Nagare, folding up his newspaper and following her. "So instead of making seven-herb porridge on the seventh of January like everyone else, they make kenoshiru soup. A huge pot of it, which they eat right through until the middle of January. Apparently the original idea was to give women a break from working in the kitchen all the time."

"Hear that, Mum?" said Koishi, kneeling in front of the family altar. "Sounds like the real gentlemen are all up in Hirosaki."

"Hey, we're even nicer in Kyoto. Kikuko knows that better than anyone."

"You keep telling yourself that, Dad," said Koishi, her eyes opening slightly as she joined her hands together and prayed.

"We'll have to make three bento boxes, won't we?" Nagare glanced at the altar, then rolled up his sleeves.

Chapter 3

Christmas Cake

1

The Karasuma-dori side of Kyoto station features an atrium in which an enormous staircase, thirty-five meters high, rises to the eleventh floor of the building. In December, the screens built into each of the 171 stairs, as well as the adjoining floors, form a gigantic Christmas light display that has become one of the city's winter attractions.

Yoshie Sakamoto made her way through the ticket gate, turned to gaze up at the staircase, and reflexively tugged on her husband Masayuki's sleeve.

"Just look at that. Beautiful, isn't it?"

"Very clever, using the stairs like that," replied Masayuki.

"What do you say we put a tree up this year?" said Yoshie, looking up at the enormous Christmas tree. Rather than replying, Masayuki simply followed her gaze in silence.

"You do know where we're going, don't you?" asked Yoshie, her breath forming white clouds in the air. She huddled closer to Masayuki, seeking protection from the icy northerly wind.

"I'm just working it out."

But even after the signal turned green, Masayuki remained rooted to the spot. Yoshie glanced sideways at him, then gently prodded him in the back. He began to walk.

They made their way north up Karasuma-dori, crossing Shichijo-dori and then turning east. They found themselves on Shomen-dori, both sides of which were lined with shops that sold Buddhist rosaries and temple robes. These had closed for the day, but amid the dark storefronts, there was one small building whose windows glowed with warm light.

"Think that's it?" asked Yoshie, pointing.

"No sign. No curtain over the entrance. Two stories, mortar walls . . . Yes, it's all just like that woman said," replied Masayuki, sliding the sheet of paper he'd been holding into his pocket.

The building didn't look much like a restaurant, and the upstairs windows were all pitch-dark. Only those on the ground floor glowed. The place looked closed, but there were definitely people inside. Yoshie and Masayuki stood at the entrance, glanced at each other, then removed their coats.

"Hello?" called Yoshie, sliding the door open.

After a brief silence, Nagare Kamogawa emerged from the kitchen in his chef's whites. "Can I help you?"

"This *is* the Kamogawa Diner, isn't it?" asked Masayuki.

"It is, but I'm afraid we've shut for the day," replied Nagare apologetically.

"Oh. We were hoping you might be able to . . . find a dish for us," said Yoshie, a pleading look in her eyes.

There was a pause.

"Well, you might as well come in." Nagare ushered them inside.

"Thank you," said the pair in unison, relief showing on their faces as they stepped into the restaurant.

Nagare pulled out two of the folding chairs. "Take a seat."

"Sorry to just turn up like this." Masayuki bowed, then sat down.

"I normally only serve food at lunchtime, you see. Evenings are for prep."

On the counter were various large trays and pots, containing what appeared to be food fresh from the kitchen. Steam was still drifting up from some of them.

Yoshie glanced at the array, then bowed deeply in Nagare's direction. "Sorry to disturb your cooking."

"That's all right." Nagare filled a Banko-ware teapot with hot water from the nearby thermos. "Where have you come from, then?"

"Fushimi," replied Yoshie. "We saw your ad in *Gourmet Monthly*."

"Ah. Not too far, then. And that one-line ad was enough for you to find us?" asked Nagare, setting two Kiyomizu-ware teacups down in front of them.

Yoshie smiled. "We phoned the publisher. At first they refused to tell us anything, but we kept pestering them until they put us through to the editor in chief."

"That Akane . . ." muttered Nagare to himself, before turning to face them. "Well, it looks like fate has brought you here."

"We're glad it did," said Masayuki, smiling.

Just then, the door to the restaurant flew open. Koishi tramped in, laden with bulging shopping bags.

"Easy!" called Nagare. "You'll scare our customers."

"Sorry," said Koishi, wincing. "Hope I didn't give you a fright."

"This is my daughter, Koishi. Technically, *she's* the one in charge of the detective agency."

The couple stood up and bowed in greeting.

"Pleased to meet you. I'm Masayuki, and this is Yoshie. We're trying to track down a certain dish and were hoping you might be able to help."

"Are you hungry?" asked Koishi. "Bet you haven't had dinner yet."

The pair's eyes lit up.

"Oh, we couldn't possibly . . ." said Yoshie, glancing sideways at Masayuki as if to gauge his reaction. "Especially after turning up out of the blue like this."

Nagare eyed them for a moment, then said, "I was just getting a few things ready for tomorrow. There's plenty to spare—just give me a moment." He bustled off to the kitchen.

"You really don't have to!" called Masayuki after him.

"Don't worry," said Koishi, pouring them some tea. "He loves serving people food."

Yoshie smiled ever so slightly. "To be honest, we *were* sort of hoping we might get to try something. That magazine editor told us your father's food is out of this world."

"Ah, so you saw the ad in *Gourmet Monthly*, then. Where are you from?"

"Fushimi," replied Yoshie tersely.

"Right. And if that's your reading material, I'm guessing you work in the food industry?"

"We run a traditional bakery," said Masayuki.

"Ooh, wagashi? I love that kind of thing," said Koishi as she sat down opposite them. "What type do you make?"

"Nothing fancy enough for use in the tea ceremony—just good old mochi cakes and bean-jam buns, mainly," said Yoshie proudly.

"Those are the best!" exclaimed Koishi, her eyes twinkling. "Let me guess: ohagi, sakura mochi . . ."

They carried on talking about traditional Japanese cakes. Eventually, Nagare emerged from the kitchen carrying a lacquered wooden tray.

Masayuki sat up in his chair. "Sorry again for barging in here like this."

"Well, I can't promise you anything too fancy." On top of the wooden tray was a pair of two-tiered Shunkei lacquerware bento boxes, their natural wood grain showing through the red lacquer.

"Oh my, is this osechi?" exclaimed Yoshie, quivering with excitement as she removed the lid from her box. "It's like the New Year has come early."

"I don't know if you can really call it that—I've just included a little bit of everything. Let me talk you through this top box. First, the sashimi: soy-marinated tuna with a wasabi dressing, fresh slices of yuba, and thin-sliced sea bream smeared with sesame-seed paste. Dashimaki omelet; miniature tilefish sushi; boiled hon-shimeji mushrooms and mizuna leaves in a bonito flake and soy sauce dressing; and pickled turnip cut into chrysanthemum flowers. These skewers are quail balls, steamed prawn, and salted smashed cucumber."

Yoshie and Masayuki listened eagerly to Nagare's explanation, licking their lips and nodding along.

"I bet some sake would go well with all this," interjected Koishi. "Shall I get you a bottle, so you can nibble on all this with a drink?"

"Believe me, we'd love to," said Masayuki, bobbing his head slightly in her direction. "But we probably shouldn't. We've got important things to discuss in a moment."

"In that case," said Nagare, "you might as well open up the lower box now too."

Yoshie nodded. She lifted her upper bento box and set it to one side, before gasping with delight at the array of food waiting below.

"The grilled dish is miso-marinated pomfret, and the small bowls are simmered Horikawa burdock with Akashi octopus, Shogoin turnip, and Donko shiitake mushrooms. Those small fish wrapped in perilla leaves are moroko, stewed in a sweet soy and mirin sauce. The deep-fried dishes are winter mackerel, done Tatsuta-age style by marinating it first, and ebi-imo taro, fried straight-up.

Wrapped around the green negi onion is roast duck; around the thicker, white negi is Kurobuta pork. Try dipping those in the wasabi or the mustard. As for the steamed rice with Seko crab, that'll taste best with these mitsuba leaves sprinkled on top. I'll bring some red miso soup with oyster tofu through in a moment. In the meantime, enjoy!"

Nagare turned and trotted back to the kitchen.

"I'll leave the tea here in case you need a top-up," said Koishi, setting a Mashiko-ware teapot down at Yoshie's side before following her father into the kitchen.

"Well. Let's tuck in!" said Masayuki.

Setting the two tiers of the large bento boxes side by side, the pair sat there for a moment, chopsticks in hand, their eyes darting from dish to dish. In the end, it was Masayuki who made the first move.

"Wow. Who knew lean tuna meat could taste this good?" he said, giving her an impressed look.

"It's even tastier than the fatty part!" exclaimed Yoshie, meeting his gaze.

"And who'd have thought sea bream would go so well with sesame-seed paste?"

"I've never had Tatsuta-age mackerel before!"

"This tilefish sushi is fantastic."

"The burdock and octopus go together wonderfully!"

They carried on sampling this dish and that, picking

up individual morsels with their chopsticks and showing them to each other.

"And here's that miso soup," said Nagare, returning with two bowls on a tray, which he set down at one end of the table.

"This food is extraordinary," said Yoshie, half rising from her seat in order to bow.

"Glad you think so," said Nagare as he positioned the bowls of soup on their wooden trays. "Take your time, now."

Masayuki smiled at him. "The craft that's gone into these dishes—it's incredible."

"Oh, I bet it's nothing compared to the amount of work that must go into your cakes. All I have to do is get my hands on decent ingredients, and the flavors take care of themselves."

"Not at all," replied Masayuki, reluctant to concede. "All *we* do is fiddle with adzuki beans and mochi all day long. I'd never be able to mix and match all these different ingredients the way you do." There was a pause before he asked, shyly, "I don't suppose there's any more of that crab rice?"

"Oh, plenty," replied Nagare.

Yoshie stared at her husband. "Masayuki! Don't be so cheeky."

"Not to worry," said Nagare. "Asking for seconds is

the biggest compliment you can pay a chef." He eyed Yoshie's bento box. "How about you? Fancy a little more rice?"

Yoshie laid a hand over the box and replied, "Oh, I've had plenty, thank you."

Nagare returned to the kitchen, and the pair continued working away at their food with their chopsticks. Sipping on the red miso soup, Masayuki turned to Yoshie.

"How many years do you think it's been since we sat down for a good meal like this, eh?"

"I wouldn't even know," replied Yoshie, gazing into the air. "Feels like the distant past."

Masayuki pressed his lips together decisively. "Well, it certainly looks like we've come to the right place."

Yoshie nodded in agreement, a smile spreading across her face.

Soon not even a single grain of rice remained in their bowls. They sat there, sipping their tea restlessly while they waited for Nagare.

"Sorry for the wait," he said when he eventually returned. "I had a few things to finish off for tomorrow."

"Not at all," said Yoshie with an apologetic shake of the head. "It's our fault for turning up unannounced."

"I'm glad you did. Seeing you polish all that food off has made my day! Now, let me show you to the office."

Nagare opened the door at the back of the room.

Following Nagare's lead, Masayuki and Yoshie slowly made their way down the long, narrow corridor that led to the rear of the restaurant.

"So this is what a proper old Kyoto house looks like—as long and narrow as an eel's bed, as they say," said Masayuki, turning around to glance at Yoshie. "Living on the outskirts of the city like we do, we don't set eyes on a place like this too often."

"The plot of land just happened to be shaped this way," Nagare said with a smile. "It isn't a proper old machiya or anything."

Yoshie, meanwhile, was gazing at the photos of food that adorned both walls of the corridor. "Are these all your creations?"

"Yes. My way of keeping track. Not very good at writing my recipes down, you see."

"We do that too," said Masayuki, pausing to inspect the photos. "Whenever we come up with a new treat, we take a photo and put it in our album."

"I've never been the organized type," said Nagare. "Which is why this place looks the way it does." He chuckled, then opened the door at the end of the corridor.

"In you come!" called Koishi from inside.

"I'll leave you to it," said Nagare, before returning to the restaurant.

Masayuki and Yoshie made their way into the room and sat down on the sofa opposite Koishi.

"Could you fill this out for me?" asked Koishi, setting her clipboard on the table between them. "Sorry, I know it's a pain."

"Can you do it?" Masayuki asked Yoshie, handing her the form before glancing at Koishi. "My handwriting's abysmal."

With the clipboard on her lap, Yoshie jotted down their details and returned it to the table.

"Yoshie and Masayuki Sakamoto," said Koishi, tracing Yoshie's neat writing with her finger. "Owners of Kogando, a Japanese bakery. I bet that's been around a long time?"

"Founded in 1928, so not *that* long ago by Kyoto standards. You have to have been around for at least a century for people here to take you seriously."

Koishi warmed to his modesty. "1928? Then you're only"—she counted on her fingers—"fifteen years off a hundred. Do you have a successor in mind?"

"Well, that's partly why we're . . ." said Masayuki. He and Yoshie exchanged a look.

Koishi adjusted her position on the sofa. "Shall we talk

about this dish, then? What is it you'd like us to help you with?

"Christmas cake," replied Yoshie shortly.

"I suppose it is that time of year, isn't it?" Koishi said, before her shoulders visibly drooped. "A cake, huh . . ."

Masayuki leaned forward. "Are cakes a no-go?"

"Not exactly. It's just . . . they're not exactly Dad's specialty." Koishi began sketching a Japanese-style Christmas cake—a sponge cake layered with whipped cream and topped with strawberries.

"I do hope you'll still be able to help us," said Yoshie, pressing her palms together imploringly.

Koishi sat up straight. "Why don't you tell me the details?"

"Well, six years ago," began Masayuki, "at about this time of year, our only son, Kakeru, died in a car accident."

There was a pause before Koishi replied, "I'm very sorry to hear that. How old was he?"

"He'd just turned ten," said Yoshie in a low voice.

"That must have been . . . a huge shock," said Koishi, studying the pair opposite as she carefully chose her words.

"It was very sudden," said Masayuki. "At first we couldn't even process it." Yoshie nodded slightly in agreement. With downcast eyes, he went on in a faltering voice.

"Our shop's near Gokonomiya Shrine, but we live a little farther out of town, so we can't really pop back to the house during the day. Kakeru was always home alone. My mother used to watch him for us, but after she fell ill, it was just him."

"He was a sensible kid," said Yoshie, taking over, "so we didn't worry too much. Then one day, when he was walking home from school with his designated group, he was hit by a car."

"I . . . see," said Koishi, barely able to get the words out.

"At the time," continued Masayuki, "there'd been a spike in road accidents involving schoolkids, and a lot of parents were insisting on picking up and dropping off their children themselves. If we'd only done the same, the poor boy would still be with us." Masayuki bit his lip.

"Well, the car that hit him was speeding, so I don't think we can really blame ourselves," said Yoshie, as if trying to convince herself. "It could just as easily have been one of us hit by that car. But for whatever reason, it was Kakeru who ended up in its path."

"Anyway," said Masayuki, steering the conversation to the topic at hand, "we only gave our son Western-style treats very rarely. It wasn't that they were banned at home or anything—it just worked out that way, seeing as we only sold Japanese confectionery. Now, Kakeru never told us this, but it seems he'd been saving up his pocket money and buying Western-style cakes every now and then. There was a cake shop in the neighborhood, you see— though it's gone out of business now."

Masayuki glanced sideways at Yoshie, who took over again. "At Kakeru's wake, the shop's owner brought a Christmas cake as an offering for the shrine." She dabbed at her eyes with a handkerchief. "That's how we found out Kakeru had been buying her cakes."

"Do you remember the name of the shop?" asked Koishi, pen at the ready.

"Cent Nuits, it was called," replied Yoshie.

"Ah. French," said Koishi, furrowing her brow slightly as she made a note.

"On the seventh day after his death," continued Yoshie, "we went to the shop to say thank you. Tiny little place, on the ground floor of an apartment building. The owner was an old lady who ran the shop single-handedly."

"Whereabouts was it?" asked Koishi, opening up a map on the table.

"Well," said Yoshie, studying the map, "if *that's* Sumizome station, and *that's* the post office . . . it was somewhere around here." She pointed at the area near a riverside temple.

"And what was the name of the old lady?" asked Koishi.

"We completely forgot to ask," replied Yoshie. "When the mourning period was over, we went there again with a card, but by then the shop had closed down."

"We were a bit of a mess at the time," explained Masayuki. "We couldn't do anything right."

"Well, let's talk about the most important part. This Christmas cake. What did it taste like?" Koishi readied her pen.

"Well," began Yoshie, exchanging a glance with Masayuki, "I only tried a single bite of the one she brought to the wake."

"I didn't eat much of it, either," murmured Masayuki.

"Oh, dear," sighed Koishi. "So it went to waste?"

"It didn't feel right, us eating the cake when she'd brought it for Kakeru. In any case, we weren't exactly in the mood for something that indulgent." Masayuki was still gazing at the location on the map.

"Oh, I can imagine. . . . Still . . ." Koishi's shoulders sagged slightly at the loss of this lead.

"I think it looked just like an ordinary Christmas cake," said Yoshie, staring off into space as she tried to remember. "Sponge cake with whipped cream and plenty of strawberries on top. I also seem to recall the base being a little firmer than the rest of it."

"There was a chocolate decoration on it too. Kakeru

loved that kind of thing." A tear ran down Masayuki's cheek. "'Merry Christmas,' it said."

"I see. And is there anything you remember about the actual taste?" Koishi glanced at each of them in turn.

"Nothing really comes to mind," said Masayuki with a vexed look.

"As I say, I only had a tiny bite, so I can't really remember, either," said Yoshie, closing her eyes to think. "But I do remember that the cream tasted rather fruity. And it was all . . . fluffy."

"Yes. The whole time it was set out at the altar, it gave off this delicious smell," added Masayuki.

Koishi's pen paused above her notebook. She appeared to be deep in thought. Yoshie and Masayuki watched her with worried expressions.

"I'm not really sure how to put this, but . . ." she began.

The couple leaned forward in unison to listen.

"If you don't remember how it tasted," Koishi went on cautiously, "then even if we manage to re-create it, how are you going to know it's the same? It all seems a little . . . pointless, if you don't mind me saying." She paused. "What made you suddenly want to try the cake *now*, after six years have gone by?"

There was a pause while silence filled the room.

"I suppose we want some kind of closure," murmured Yoshie, her eyes fixed on the low table in front of her.

"Yes," continued Masayuki. "It seems to us that, well, if we could just taste this cake he was so fond of, we might be able to put all this behind us."

"You mean you want to forget?"

"Forget Kakeru?" replied Masayuki sharply. "How could we? No, we'll never forget him, whatever happens." His eyes were moist with tears.

"But we do need to move on somehow," continued Yoshie. "It's been rather a long time."

"Yes. We can't go on like this," said Masayuki. He seemed to be addressing himself more than anyone else. "We just can't."

He said these last words with such forcefulness that no one seemed able to break the ensuing silence.

"The shop's been in our family for generations. I'm the fourth," he eventually continued, in a restrained voice. Koishi waited for him to go on. "And at this rate, I'll be the last," he said, gazing up at the ceiling. "Now, until a couple of years ago, I was fine with that. I convinced myself my forebears would forgive me if I chose to bow out now."

"But there's this student," said Yoshie. "A boy with a bit of a sweet tooth. He pops by our shop every now and then to buy something. He's graduating from Kyonan University this spring, and, well . . ."

Yoshie glanced at Masayuki, as if urging him to continue.

"Katsuya, the kid's name is," said Masayuki, his expression brightening ever so slightly. "He's got a thing for Japanese cakes. Drops by at least once a week to stock up. A couple of weeks ago, just as he was leaving the shop, he suddenly asked if he we'd take him on as an apprentice."

"Wow," said Koishi. "So he really does love his cakes."

"With a degree from Kyonan, he could probably land a job at any of the big companies. But it seems he has other ideas," Masayuki said, grinning.

"Meanwhile," said Yoshie, "we've no idea how long we'll be able to keep running the shop."

"What's his full name?" asked Koishi.

"Katsuya Aso," replied Yoshie. "He's twenty-two."

"And you're thinking he could become the fifth generation to run the shop?" Koishi looked steadily at the couple.

"Well, that's all still a long way off," sighed Masayuki, "but it's something we should consider before taking him on. To be honest, we're not sure what to do. It would feel a bit like giving up on Kakeru, you see."

"We just don't quite feel ready," added Yoshie, straightening her posture.

"And if we managed to re-create that Christmas cake for you, and you were to eat it, that would help you make your mind up. Is that what you're saying?" asked Koishi.

They shook their heads vaguely. "I'm not sure it's that simple," said Yoshie.

Koishi paused, unsure how to continue.

"In any case," said Masayuki, "Yoshie and I have spent the last couple of weeks thinking everything over, and the answer we keep arriving at is that cake. I know it might seem a little strange, but please—we need your help." He stood up and bowed deeply. Yoshie glanced at him, then hurriedly followed suit.

"Right, then," said Koishi, closing her notebook. "I'll make sure Dad knows just what's at stake."

"Thank you," said the pair in unison, bowing again.

Back in the restaurant, Nagare smiled as if he'd been eagerly awaiting their return.

"All sorted?"

Yoshie returned his smile. "We gave her the whole story."

"Glad to hear it."

"Dad, this one's going to take some serious investigating."

The look of relief that had come across Nagare's face was immediately replaced by an anxious frown.

"We're asking rather a lot, I'm afraid," said Masayuki, bowing his head.

"Whatever it is, I'll do my best not to let you down."

"Thank you," said Yoshie, making a bow of her own.

"Koishi, did you make an appointment for next time?"

"Oops!" exclaimed Koishi, before turning to the couple. "Um, how does two weeks from today sound?"

"Two weeks from today is the twenty-fourth," remarked Nagare, glancing at the calendar on the wall. "I don't imagine you'll want to spend Christmas Eve here, will you?"

The couple glanced at each other and shook their heads, then turned to face Koishi. "It's not a problem for us," said Yoshie, "but what about you, Koishi? Isn't that when young ladies like you go out on a date?"

"You don't need to worry about her," said Nagare. "Every year it's just the two of us sitting around a hot pot."

"Shush, Dad." Koishi forced a smile as she turned to the couple. "But yes, you're more than welcome."

"And how much do we owe you for that meal?" asked Yoshie, extracting her wallet from her handbag.

"You can pay us later, together with the detective fee," replied Nagare.

They bowed and thanked him again, then made their way out of the restaurant.

"Take care, now," said Nagare, standing outside with Koishi to see them off. Once they'd disappeared from view, he blew into his hands to warm them. "It's gotten chilly."

"I really think this might be the hardest one yet, Dad," said Koishi as they made their way back inside.

"What's the dish?"

"Christmas cake."

"C-Christmas cake?" repeated Nagare, bewildered.

Koishi had opened her notebook, but now she clapped it shut again. "Do you think we should turn them down?"

"Are you joking? Of course not. We'll find a way. Now, what sort of cake are we talking about?" He reached for the notebook and, settling into one of the folding chairs, begin flipping through its pages. "Cent . . . Nuits? Looks like I'll have to work on my French first."

"Dad," murmured Koishi. "Part of me feels like it might be best if you *don't* find this one."

"Why's that?" asked Nagare, his eyes still on the notebook. Koishi gave him a brief rundown of the circumstances behind the request.

"Listen, Koishi," said Nagare, looking up as he interrupted her. "Our job is to re-create the dishes that people ask us to find. We don't concern ourselves with what happens afterward. That's not for us to decide."

Koishi looked at him for a moment, then gave a brief nod of understanding.

2

It felt as though the Christmas music had followed them all the way from their doorway to Kyoto station. When they caught their fingers and feet tapping along to the beat, Masayuki and Yoshie could only laugh.

"Remember when Kakeru figured out that Santa was really just you in disguise?" asked Yoshie as they approached the Kamogawa Diner.

"Oh, do I ever." Masayuki smiled. *"So it was you all along!* There can't be many parents who'd keep their cool when their five-year-old comes out with something like that."

"Sneaking a look when you were putting the presents by his pillow—that was just like him, wasn't it?"

Yoshie looked up at the restaurant. Was that a Christmas tree in the second-floor window? Through the lace curtains, she thought she could glimpse various other colorful decorations too.

"Oh yes," said Masayuki. "There was no hiding anything

from that kid." He glanced up at the window too, then raised his eyes to the thick clouds blanketing the sky.

A tabby cat appeared as if from nowhere and, after curling itself around their legs, offered a single *meow* in greeting.

"Where did you come from, eh?" asked Yoshie, squatting to stroke it on the head.

"Oh, he's ours," said Koishi, emerging from the restaurant and crouching down alongside her. "We called him Drowsy because all he ever does is sleep."

Masayuki looked puzzled. "He wasn't here last time we came by, was he? You'd think we'd have at least heard him meowing somewhere."

"Dad won't let him into the restaurant," replied Koishi, cradling the cat in her arms and getting to her feet. "Says he can't have a cat running around while he's serving people food. So Drowsy spends a lot of his time at our neighbor's house."

"It's the same at our place. When I was little, I always thought we could at least have a pet at home, seeing as the shop was on separate premises. But my father said he couldn't risk a single hair getting in his cakes—so no dog for me." Masayuki's voice grew quieter as he went on. "When Kakeru tried to bring a puppy home one day, I found myself telling him the same thing."

"It's cold out here. Why don't you come on in?" asked Koishi, setting the cat down and sliding the door open.

"I guess this is goodbye for now, Drowsy!" said Yoshie. She gave him a reluctant wave as she followed her husband inside.

"Smells like a cake shop in here!" exclaimed Masayuki with a grin.

"Our customers have been telling us that too," chuckled Koishi. "They keep asking if we're planning on switching professions."

"I've been baking round the clock," said Nagare as he arrived from the kitchen. "Thanks for coming back."

"Oh, dear. We've really put you through the wringer, haven't we?" said Yoshie, folding up her coat and bowing.

"Not at all. It's our job! Please, take a seat." At his urging, the pair sat down.

"Meanwhile," said Koishi as she laid a red gingham cloth over the table, "I'm in charge of making things feel nice and Christmassy."

"Koishi," said Nagare, "don't tell me you've forgotten the tree?"

"Oops! I'll be right back." She trotted off into the kitchen, and they heard her ascending the stairs. Yoshie remembered the tree she had glimpsed in the window.

"I managed to track down this cake you ate," said Nagare, "but making it from scratch turned out to be quite a challenge. I mean, I've never baked a cake in my life! Still, this morning, I think I finally cracked it. I'll just fetch it." He ducked under the curtain separating the restaurant from the kitchen.

The ensuing silence was soon broken by the sound of footsteps tramping down the stairs. A moment later, Koishi burst back into the restaurant, bundling the Christmas tree in her arms.

"Sorry to make such a scene!" she called as she scanned the room for somewhere to put it.

Masayuki got up from his chair. "You really don't have to do all this."

"Oh, yes we do. Now . . ." Koishi slipped behind him and positioned the tree by the wall. "There we go."

Yoshie smiled. "We got a tree this year too—our first for a while. They *are* nice, aren't they?"

"Can I get you a hot drink?" asked Koishi, straightening out the tablecloth. "We have coffee, black tea, green tea. . . ."

"Green tea, please," replied Yoshie. "We're not so used to Western drinks." Masayuki nodded in agreement.

"Japanese tea all the way, is it? Are all wagashi makers like that?"

Masayuki smiled slightly. "I suppose it's the same with

most traditional artisans, yes. At the more modern places, it's a different story."

"Koishi, can you get the small plates out?" Nagare appeared beside the table, holding a silver tray in both hands just above eye level, as if making an offering. On it, perched on a white plate, was the Christmas cake.

"You've even used Western crockery. Very appropriate," remarked Yoshie.

"Nothing beats these white Ginori plates," said Nagare. "The forks are from the same brand too." He set the cake down in front of them.

Masayuki leaned forward and inspected the cake from above. "So this is it, eh. . . ."

"Yes," replied Nagare, gazing at the cake. "The Christmas cake that the woman gave in offering to your son."

Yoshie's nose twitched. "The smell . . . I remember the smell!"

Koishi positioned a Mashiko-ware teapot on the table. "I went with roasted green tea in the end, but perhaps you'd have preferred unroasted?"

"No, hojicha is perfect," said Masayuki with a faint smile.

"I'll leave the knife here. Please, eat it however you like." Nagare stowed the tray under his arm, then bowed and vanished into the kitchen.

"I brewed plenty, but just let me know if you need a

refill." Koishi filled two Karatsu teacups from the pot, then followed her father out of the room.

For a moment, Yoshie and Masayuki sat opposite each other, facing the plate without moving a muscle.

The cake, about twenty centimeters in diameter, was covered with whipped cream and topped with a layer of strawberries, among which nestled a marzipan Santa and a large chocolate star.

"So this is it," said Masayuki.

"Yes," said Yoshie. "I suppose it is."

They continued simply gazing at the cake.

After a few minutes, Masayuki seemed to summon up his resolve and reached for the cake knife. He positioned the tip of the blade in the center of the cake. Then, still gripping it firmly, he froze. A light sweat had formed on his brow.

"It's no good," he said, handing the knife to Yoshie. "Can you do it?"

"I just . . . wish he could have seen this." Her eyes swelled with tears as she grasped the knife.

Masayuki's cheeks were also wet with tears. "Let's take it home with us. We can put it by his altar for a while first and eat it later. It just doesn't feel right, does it? Eating something this delicious without giving him a chance to try it first."

"Ah, I meant to say," said Nagare, poking his head

through the curtain. "I made another one for you to leave by Kakeru's altar. So you can tuck in with a clear conscience." He disappeared back into the kitchen.

"It's like he can read our minds," said Masayuki, wiping the tears from his eyes.

"Well, I suppose we should do as he says."

Yoshie inserted the knife into the cake. She felt it slide effortlessly through the cream and sponge before encountering a slight resistance at the base of the cake.

"It's a lot firmer at the bottom," said Yoshie, placing a slice onto each of the two small plates.

"It really does smell good, doesn't it?" said Masayuki, leaning in to sniff the cake as he readied his fork. In the meantime, Yoshie had already taken her first bite.

"Mmm!"

"Wow," said Masayuki, his entire face creasing into a smile as he followed suit. "Delicious."

As they chewed, they gazed down at the slices of cake in front of them.

"Well, how is it?" asked Nagare, appearing at their side with a Kyo-ware teapot. "Taste the same?"

"To be honest," said Masayuki, "I don't remember well enough to be able to tell you. But I have a feeling it was . . . something like this, yes." He nodded several times as he spoke.

"I think it's coming back to me," said Yoshie, closing

her eyes. "The smell, the taste—and most of all, this texture. Yes, it was just like this."

"That's a relief," said Nagare, replacing their teacups and filling the new ones with unroasted green tea.

Masayuki dabbed his mouth with a handkerchief. "But how did you manage it?"

"At first," said Nagare, smiling as he clutched the teapot, "I thought it'd be a cinch. I mean, I didn't even have to leave Kyoto! But it all turned out a little trickier than I'd expected."

"I can imagine," said Masayuki, gesturing for Nagare to join them at the table. "We tried asking around the neighborhood ourselves, but no one had a clue where the woman who ran that cake shop had gone."

Nagare sat down and placed his notebook on the table. "She wasn't a member of the Cake Shop Association, so that was a dead end. I was beginning to think it was hopeless—and then I remembered the name of the shop. Cent Nuits."

"Dad's French is hopeless," said Koishi, emerging from the kitchen and standing behind Nagare. "I had to give him a hand."

"Much appreciated," said Yoshie, bowing slightly in her direction.

"Apparently it means 'a hundred nights,'" said Nagare. "That struck me as an odd name for a cake shop—and then it hit me. See, the shop was located in the Fukakusa neighborhood of Fushimi. That made me think of one of its more famous residents—the legendary Fukakusa no Shosho. Now, do you remember the name of the story he's famous for? 'A Hundred Nights.'"

Nagare laid a photo on the table. Taken in Fukakusa, it showed two stone memorial towers dedicated to Fukakusa no Shosho and his beloved, the beautiful poet Ono no Komachi.

"Ah, yes," said Masayuki, eagerly inspecting the photo. "It's a wonderful story. Slightly different ending from the Noh version, though."

"In the Noh play," said Nagare, "both Komachi and Shosho are saved through the grace of Buddha. But that version is set in the northern part of Kyoto, so there wouldn't be much of a connection with a shop down south in Fukakusa."

Yoshie looked dubious. "Mr. Kamogawa, this is all just a theory on your part, isn't it?"

"Dad's theories usually turn out right," said Koishi proudly.

"True, it was no more than a guess—at first." Nagare's expression became pensive. "Sad old story, isn't it? Ono no Komachi, famed for her poetry and beauty, promises Fukakusa no Shosho she'll marry him if he visits her for a hundred nights in a row. He does exactly as she says, dutifully visiting her deep into the winter—but on the final night, he freezes to death in the snow. That's the story, anyway. And it turns out Satoko Oshima named her cake shop after it."

Masayuki leaned forward. "So that's her name? How did you find out?"

Nagare opened a Kyoto guidebook on the table. "There I was, at my wit's end. Not a clue in sight. I was flicking through this guidebook aimlessly when a certain establishment caught my attention. A cake shop called Ninety-Nine Nights."

Nagare flicked to the page on the Kyoto imperial garden and pointed to the accompanying guide to nearby shops. Yoshie and Masayuki looked dumbfounded.

"Ninety-nine?" asked Koishi.

"I figured there had to be some sort of connection, so I paid the place a visit. It turned out I was right. The shop was run by a pâtissier named Kaori Oshima, who turned out to be Satoko's granddaughter. Apparently she'd helped out at Cent Nuits when she was younger, then ended up opening her own place."

Nagare set a photo of Satoko on the table.

"Yes, that's the old lady!" said Yoshie, reaching for the photo. "Such elegant white hair. And that gentle look on her face."

"Kaori remembered young Kakeru's weekly visits well.

It seems Satoko was very fond of him. Talked his ear off whenever he dropped by, apparently."

"That's our Kakeru," said Masayuki, his eyes growing moist again. "He always was a good listener for his age."

"There must have been all sorts he wanted to tell us," added Yoshie, sniffling loudly. "But he'd always just sit there patiently, listening to us grumble about this or that."

"Now," said Nagare, getting back to his story. "It seems this cake comes with an American twist. One with a deep connection to the Fukakusa neighborhood."

"An . . . American twist?" asked Masayuki.

"After the war, American troops were stationed in Fukakusa. They had a headquarters in what is now Ryukoku University, on the first floor of the old library. Satoko, who had studied abroad and spoke good English, managed to get a job there as an interpreter. She was regularly invited to one of the officers' houses, where she ended up learning how to bake American-style cakes. Later, she ran a cake-making school at her own apartment. Then, around ten years ago, she finally opened her own little shop, open just three days a week. Since it was on the way to school, the sharp-eyed Kakeru couldn't fail to spot it."

Nagare showed them a photo of the cake shop in its prime.

"Apparently that crunchy bottom layer is called a 'biscuit base' in English," Koishi chimed in. "Wheat flour dough mixed with lard, and leavened with baking soda."

Yoshie scooped some of the cake's topping onto her finger. "This cream. Why does it smell so good?"

"Satoko mixed peach juice into it. Fushimi used to be famous for peaches, after all—I mean, the Momoyama castle was even named after them."

Yoshie nodded. "It all makes sense."

"One more night, and he would have reached a hundred," said Masayuki soberly, his thoughts returning to Fukakusa. "After all that effort. The poor man must have been consumed by regret."

Nagare looked evenly back at him. "He never managed to fulfill his vow, it's true. But it's his devotion that people remember. I think that's why Satoko named her shop after him—and why Kaori chose to follow her lead."

Masayuki gazed back at Nagare without saying a word.

"Shall I brew us some more tea?" said Koishi, apparently unable to bear the silence.

"We should probably be going, thank you," said Yoshie, glancing at Masayuki as she rose from her chair. "We want to offer that cake to Kakeru as soon as possible."

"Ah, yes," said Nagare, getting up and making for the kitchen. "Can't keep him waiting."

"Now, what do we owe you?" said Masayuki, getting out his wallet.

Koishi passed him a slip of paper. "Whatever you feel is right. Just send it to this account when you have a moment."

"Right, then," said Masayuki, tucking the slip into his wallet.

"I don't imagine you'll be in a rush to bake it yourselves," said Nagare, reappearing at their side, "but I've included the recipe just in case. As passed down to Kaori by Satoko. Ah, and she gave me something else too—something very important." He reached into the paper bag he was holding and produced a small framed drawing, which he handed to Masayuki. "Kakeru gave it to Satoko as a present. She liked it so much she had it framed."

"Why, that's our Sakuragawa cake!" exclaimed Masayuki, showing the drawing to Yoshie. "Look. He's captured it so well."

"He really has," she replied, her eyes glistening again as she turned to Nagare. "We used to bring home the leftover cakes for him to eat, you see."

"Apparently he told Satoko he couldn't bring her a real one, so he drew her this instead," said Nagare.

"It's our most popular cake," continued Yoshie tearfully. "Named after the Noh play. There's a wonderful old Noh stage at Gokonomiya Shrine, you see, just around the corner from the shop. The recipe for the cake has been passed down for three generations."

"So Kakeru was doing his bit to promote your business, then," said Koishi. Her voice was catching slightly in her throat too.

"We'll treasure this," said Masayuki, carefully returning the picture to the paper bag.

Yoshie bowed deeply at his side. "Thank you for everything."

As Nagare slid the door to the restaurant open, he noticed that his breath was white in the air. "It's nippy out here. I think we might have snow tonight."

"Ooh," said Koishi. "White Christmas, you reckon?" She bent down to pick up Drowsy, who had trotted over to join them.

"You take care of yourself, you hear?" said Yoshie to the cat, patting it on the head.

Masayuki straightened his back. "We're going to visit the family grave tomorrow. We intend to tell Kakeru and our forebears about the plan to take Katsuya on as an apprentice."

"Ah. Very good," said Nagare.

The couple thanked them again, bowed, and set off down Shomen-dori.

"Oh, one more thing!" called Nagare. They stopped and turned. "Remember what Zeami said: 'The true legacy lies not in the name, but in the teaching.'"

Masayuki nodded, then brought his palms together at his chest and bowed once more.

Once the couple had disappeared from view, Koishi and Nagare retreated inside. Drowsy, apparently reluctant to part ways, mewed plaintively after them.

"What on earth was that, Dad?" asked Koishi as she removed the tablecloth. "It sounded like you were putting a curse on them or something."

"What are you talking about? It's from the famous ending to *Style and the Flower*. You know, by the great playwright Zeami."

"My French might be better than yours, but Noh theater isn't exactly my strong suit. What does it mean, then?"

"He's saying that an artistic lineage doesn't always have to be passed on by blood," said Nagare as he cleared away the plates and ducked under the curtain to the kitchen. "What counts is passing on your art, in its every detail, to whoever picks up the baton. Something like that, anyway."

"Sounds a little complicated," said Koishi, wiping the table down. "You sure those two will understand?"

"Koishi, they named one of their cakes after a Noh

play," replied Nagare over the counter. "I think they should just about get it."

Koishi had finished cleaning up and settled herself at the counter. "What's that play about, then?"

"*Sakura-Gawa*? It's a very sad story," said Nagare as he set a pot on the stove. "About a daughter who's separated from her mother at a young age."

"Oh. Talk about touching a nerve! Why would they name a cake after something so sad?"

"Don't worry, it has a happy ending. The mother and daughter are finally reunited."

Nagare took a slice of cake, then made his way into the living room, where he sat in front of the altar and set it down in offering. Koishi hurried over and kneeled at his side.

"Knowing Kikuko, she's probably looking for Kakeru right now."

"Hey, Mum," said Koishi, joining her hands together in prayer. "If you find him, share a slice of this with him, okay?"

"The three of us never got a chance to eat Christmas cake together, did we?" said Nagare in the direction of the altar.

"You always said you were too busy at that time of year," said Koishi, her voice turning somber. "It was just the two of us—wasn't it, Mum?"

"Mum says she's had enough cake, and bring on the sake."

"Hey!" chuckled Koishi. "Stop putting words in her mouth."

Laughing even as they sniffed back tears, Koishi and Nagare gazed up at the altar.

Chapter 4

Fried Rice

1

As a model, she was used to catching people's attention, but this was something else.

With her black cashmere coat and chestnut hair rippling in the wind, and a designer patent-leather handbag dangling from her shoulder, Hatsuko Shirasaki was strutting her way down the Kyoto streets. In Tokyo, she would have blended right in, but against the backdrop of Higashi Honganji temple, or the shops on Shomen-dori selling Buddhist paraphernalia, she cut quite the unusual figure. Her bold looks and slim, tall figure turned the head of every passerby. Eventually she grew so self-conscious that she could only stare down at the pavement—with the result that when she reached her destination, it took her a moment to realize she'd arrived.

A tabby cat approached her, mewing softly.

"Hello, you," said Hatsuko, squatting and gently stroking the cat's forehead. "Drowsy, was it?"

"Hatsuko!" exclaimed Koishi, rushing out to meet her.

"Been a while, hasn't it?" replied Hatsuko, getting to her feet. "I've come to see your dad about something," she added with a grin.

"Well, come on in. Sorry the place is a bit of a mess." Koishi slid the door open and ushered her inside, stealing a glance at her outfit as she did so.

"See you later, Drowsy!" said Hatsuko with a wave.

"How many years has it been, do you think?" asked Koishi, showing her to a chair.

"I'm in Kyoto often enough for work," replied Hatsuko, removing her coat, "but I haven't seen *you* since . . ." She looked up at the ceiling as if trying to remember.

"Akemi's wedding, maybe? Well, you're looking as stunning as ever!" Koishi was gazing at her as though transfixed.

"I could say the same about you. The pride of Nishiyama University—and you haven't changed a bit."

"Are you kidding?" said Koishi, before shrugging. "These days, 'dowdy middle-aged waitress' is closer to the mark."

A man was sitting at the counter, facing away from them. "Thanks for the soba," he said, getting to his feet. "Delicious as always!"

"You're welcome, Hiroshi," called Nagare from the kitchen. "Sure you've had enough?"

"Plenty." Hiroshi grinned, slapping a five-hundred-yen coin on the counter. "That kudzu starch you put in the broth makes it extra filling. Really hits the spot."

"Hey, it's cold out there. Take care!" said Koishi.

"You too," he said, patting her on the shoulder as he made his way out of the restaurant.

Hatsuko gave Koishi a meaningful look. "Someone special?"

"Of course not!" Koishi said, blushing. "Hiroshi's just . . . a customer. He runs a sushi place around the corner."

"Well, you always did like your sushi. . . ." replied Hatsuko, studying her intently.

"Is that really Hatsuko I hear?" called Nagare, wiping his hands as he walked out from the kitchen in his apron.

"Nagare!" said Hatsuko, bobbing her head in his direction.

"Funny, I see you so often in magazines that it only feels like a few days since we last met. You seem to be doing very well for yourself—unlike certain other people your age. . . ."

"Seriously, Dad?" huffed Koishi. "Anyway, Hatsuko, you must be hungry."

"Well," said Hatsuko, "that ad *did* say 'Kamogawa Diner,' so I was hoping there might be something tasty on the menu." She grinned mischievously. "I've barely eaten today."

"She's here for the detective service, Dad," said Koishi. "Dish her up something tasty, all right? I'll take care of the interview."

"Don't worry. I'll whip up something special for your talented friend—just give me a moment." Nagare hurried off to the kitchen.

"I'm impressed you found us," said Koishi, filling a teapot with tea leaves. "We still lived over in Shichiku when you used to drop by, didn't we?"

"You told me you'd moved at Akemi's wedding, remember? To somewhere nearer the station."

"That's right. We keep this place a bit of a secret, for various reasons."

"I had a brain wave when I saw that ad in *Gourmet Monthly*," continued Hatsuko, glancing around the restaurant. "*Kamogawa Diner—Kamogawa Detective Agency — We Find Your Food*. I just *knew* it had to be you and your dad."

"You always were a sharp one," said Koishi as she filled the Kyo-ware teapot with hot water.

"And where's your mum's altar?"

"In the living room," said Koishi, nodding toward the back of the restaurant.

"Can I pay my respects?"

"Of course."

Koishi showed Hatsuko to the tatami-matted room. "You were like a daughter to Mum, you know," she said, her voice quivering slightly. "She didn't care if we were the same age—I was the little baby, and you my big sister."

Hatsuko kneeled, lit a stick of incense, and placed it in front of the altar. "She always used to give me advice. 'Never trust a man who tries to win you over with cheap tricks,' she used to say."

"Oh yes." Koishi pouted. "She always used to say you were the type to be tricked, whereas I was the trickster. Character assassination, that's what it was!"

Hatsuko got to her feet. "She was probably just worried about me. I mean, I *did* move here from the sticks."

"Oh, *sure*!" replied Koishi as they made their way back into the restaurant. "You could ask a hundred people to guess which of us is the country bumpkin, and they'd all say it was me."

Hatsuko simply chuckled in response.

"That laugh of yours hasn't changed since your student days," said Nagare, arriving from the kitchen. "Well, here we are. A meal fit for a princess—even if it's just a bento. I've done it Shokado-style, divided into four sections." As he set the lidded, black lacquered box on the table, Hatsuko hurried over and took her seat at the table.

"I always thought your specialty was eating food rather than cooking it, Nagare. But it sounds like you're a real pro in the kitchen!"

"Go on, take the lid off."

"The dramatic reveal, huh?" Using both hands, Hatsuko carefully opened up the lid—then gasped with delight. "But this is . . . high-end cuisine!" Her eyes darted excitedly around the box. "And there you were, calling it 'just a bento.'"

"Oh, I'm not sure it'll be up to your standards. You're always eating much fancier stuff in the magazines."

Nagare folded his arms and gazed at Hatsuko as she surveyed the meal.

"Don't just gawp at her, Dad," needled Koishi. "You haven't explained what's in it."

"Ah . . . yes," said Nagare, refocusing his gaze on the contents of the bento. "Shokado bento boxes were originally paint boxes, you know—that's why they're divided up into squares like that. Anyway, in the top left are the appetizers. Wakasa winter mackerel, marinated in vinegar and served sashimi-style; Hinase oysters simmered in a sweet soy and mirin sauce; Kyoto-reared chicken, deep-fried in the Toji temple style using a yuba batter; vinegared Taiza crab; stewed Shishigatani pumpkin; and Omi beef, marinated and deep-fried Tatsuta-age style. All served bite-size. In the top right is what we call 'imobo'—

dried codfish stewed with ebi-imo taro. I've served it with grated yuzu from Mio. Should brighten up the flavor a little. Bottom right is a selection of sashimi: lightly salted Wakasa tilefish served on a bed of kelp, and Toyama winter yellowtail, sliced extra thin and wrapped in thin slices of lightly pickled Shogoin turnip. Try those with a bit of the shredded shio-kombu—kelp simmered in soy sauce. And bottom left is the rice, cooked in soft-shelled turtle broth. It's a very delicate flavor, so you can eat it just like you would plain white rice. In that little sake cup is some squeezed ginger juice—try drizzling that on the rice, if you like. It'll really bring out the flavor. The soup is white miso with chunks of millet cake. Take your time, and enjoy!"

Nagare, who had barely paused for breath, disappeared into the kitchen with his tray. Koishi patted Hatsuko gently on the shoulder, then followed him.

With her hands clasped neatly in her lap, Hatsuko stared in wonder at the array of dishes in front of her. She thought she could hear Drowsy mewling softly outside the restaurant.

A minute or so later, she finally pressed her palms together, then reached for her chopsticks. First she tried the salted tilefish sashimi. She garnished it with some of the shredded shio-kombu and a dab of a wasabi, then slipped it into her mouth.

After a small gasp of pleasure, she moved on to her next target, positioning some of the deep-fried beef on the turtle-broth rice. As she chewed, a smile of delight began to spread across her face. It only grew wider when she tried the simmered oysters, the vinegared mackerel, and the ever-so-delicate imobo. As she sampled dish after dish, her mouth filled with rich flavors.

"Need a refill?" asked Koishi, appearing at her side with a Banko teapot.

"Please," said Hatsuko, holding out her Karatsu-ware teacup. "Koishi, I had no idea your dad was such a whiz in the kitchen. This food is incredible!"

"Really?" said Koishi, beaming as she finished pouring the tea. "Even by your standards? Well, that's a relief. Dad and I were biting our nails next door."

"*My standards*, huh? I guess people do judge you based on what they eat, don't they?"

"We can talk about all that in a moment. For now, just enjoy the meal. Would you like me to bring some sake?"

"You know, I think I would," said Hatsuko in an indulgent voice.

"Drank like a fish back in the day, didn't you?" Koishi grinned, making for the kitchen with the teapot. "Shall I warm it up for you?"

"Please. But not too much."

"Yes, *madam*," Koishi chuckled as she turned. "You really haven't changed a bit, you know."

Hatsuko picked up her chopsticks again and turned her attention to the yellowtail sashimi. The thin slices of fish glistened in their white turnip sheaths. A liberal dollop of wasabi, a sprinkle of the shredded shio-kombu, and they were ready for consumption. The briny tang of the fish contrasted pleasantly with the refreshing coolness of the turnip. Hatsuko sat bolt upright in her chair, savoring the taste.

"You always did prefer your sake warm, didn't you?" said Nagare, placing a Bizen ceramic sake bottle and a small blue Kutani cup in front of her. "Used to really swig it down whenever you came over."

"Sorry. I bet I was a real nuisance." Hatsuko bowed her head slightly as she held the sake cup for Nagare to fill.

"You don't know how relieved I am that you liked the food," said Nagare, casting an eye over the near-depleted bento box. "I know it's not the most exciting cuisine."

Hatsuko's expression turned serious. "Not exciting? What are you talking about? This is the kind of proper Kyoto food I hardly ever get the chance to eat!"

"That's very kind of you, Hatsuko, but I'd hardly call this authentic Kyoto cooking. It's not like I learned it from a master chef or anything. I just tinker around, really."

"First you were a police detective—now you're edging toward culinary perfection. You're basically Superman."

"I *really* don't know about that," said Nagare, scratching his head.

"No need to blush, Dad," said Koishi, prodding him from behind. "She's just being nice."

"No, I mean it," said Hatsuko with a slight pout.

"Koishi, how's she supposed to enjoy her meal with us standing here?" said Nagare, tugging on his daughter's sleeve. "Let's leave her to it."

"Just let me know if that sake needs topping up!" Koishi called over her shoulder as she was hustled into the kitchen.

Hatsuko took a long, considered sip from the cobalt-blue sake cup. Once the warm liquid had trickled down her throat, she let out a quiet sigh of contentment.

She reached again for her chopsticks, this time extracting a piece of the Toji-style fried chicken. She chewed it slowly, savoring the fragrant yuba batter, then took another sip of the warm sake. Then she repeated this procedure, alternating between chopsticks and sake cup, until the bento box was completely empty. She shook the sake bottle; there was still a little left. Normally it was the other way around: she'd finish her drink but leave food on her plate.

Hatsuko found herself thinking of the last time she'd eaten with her father. She'd still been in primary school at the time, so her memory of the occasion was a little vague. They'd eaten at an elegant ryotei restaurant—a rarity in the rural area where she'd grown up. Looking back now, she realized it must have been where her father took important clients. He'd even been on friendly terms with the elderly kimonoed waitress. Sashimi, tempura, steak—everything they'd eaten must have been luxury cuisine of the finest quality. And yet, in her memory, none of it tasted particularly good.

After they'd finished the main course, her father had cried over the melon that was served as dessert. Of course, *he* had known it was the last meal they would share, but young Hatsuko had been completely in the dark. Now, twiddling her empty sake cup in her fingers, she gazed up at the ceiling of the Kamogawa Diner.

"Shall I open another bottle?" asked Nagare, appearing with his tray tucked under one shoulder.

"No, thanks. That was plenty." Hatsuko pressed her hands together in gratitude.

"Koishi's just getting ready in the office at the back," said Nagare as he replaced the lid on the bento box. I'll show you through after you've had a moment to digest."

"Thanks. And Nagare," Hatsuko went on, looking up

at him sincerely, "that really was an amazing meal. I'm not just saying that."

"Oh, I know," replied Nagare, meeting her gaze. "You're not the type to go around flattering people without good reason—I know that better than anyone."

"My talent agency is always telling me I have to make a good impression on people if I really want to make it."

"Well, I don't think you need to worry about being anyone but yourself."

Lowering her gaze to the table, she seemed to mull his words.

"Fancy some tea?" Nagare asked. "Might help clear your head after the sake."

"No, I'm fine," said Hatsuko. "Could you show me through to Koishi?"

Nagare guided her down the corridor that led to the rear of the restaurant, her heels clicking quietly as she followed.

"In you come!" said Koishi, smiling through the doorway at the end of the corridor.

"I'm counting on you, Koishi," said Nagare, before returning to the restaurant.

Hatsuko bowed slightly as she entered the room.

"Easier to talk here than in the restaurant, don't you think?" Koishi said, then gestured toward the sofa. "Go on, take a seat."

"I love the retro interior. And the garden view!" Hatsuko glanced around the room, then slowly settled herself on the sofa.

"I know it's a little formal, but could you fill this out for me?" said Koishi, sitting down opposite her and sliding a clipboard across the table. "We take record-keeping very seriously, you see."

"You're making me nervous!" said Hatsuko, resting the clipboard on her lap as she filled it out.

"Never thought I'd see *you* on the other side of this table," said Koishi, gazing at her friend's hand as she wrote.

Hatsuko returned the clipboard. "Will that do, detective?"

"Oh, I should think so." Koishi opened her notebook. "Well then, Hatsuko Shirasaki, what's the dish you'd like us to re-create?"

"Fried rice."

"Fried . . . rice?" Koishi's eyes seemed to bulge with shock. "*You* want us to make you . . . fried rice?"

"What's wrong with that?"

"It's just that, what with you being a model and everything, I thought it might be something a little . . . flashier."

Hatsuko sighed and looked up at the ceiling.

"I mean," continued Koishi, "in the magazines, you're always going to fancy restaurants and eating luxury French cuisine, or Michelin-starred Italian food. . . ."

"You know I was born in Shikoku, don't you? The complete middle of nowhere. I lived there until I was ten, when, because of . . . this and that, my uncle in Kyoto took me in. But the dish I want to eat is the fried rice my mum made for me when I was little." Hatsuko spoke slowly, as if choosing her words with great care.

"Your childhood has always been off-limits. But if we're going to try and re-create that fried rice, I'm going to need a few more details." Koishi glanced up at her with a pleading look. "Will that be okay?"

"My agency doesn't really like me talking about my upbringing, either. But . . ." She straightened her posture. "I trust you, Koishi."

"You have nothing to worry about. We're friends—and anyway, detectives are sworn to secrecy."

"Thanks." Hatsuko bowed her head, then took a long sip from the teacup in front of her before she went on. "I was born in Ehime prefecture, in a fishing town called Yawatahama. Just after I turned ten, the local company where my dad worked went bust. My mum had always struggled with illness, and the anxiety of it all was too much for her. She passed away soon afterward." Hatsu-ko's voice had dropped to a murmur.

"Would you mind telling me your parents' names?"

"My father is Fumio Shirasaki; my mother was Yas-uyo."

"What happened to your father afterward?"

"Well, it turned out he'd been involved in cooking the company's books. He was sentenced to a hefty fine. That was when he asked my uncle to take me in. I guess he barely felt able to look out for himself, never mind his daughter. After that, he started working as a . . . seasonal laborer, I guess you'd call it. Moving around the country to wherever the work was."

"That must have been so hard for you."

"Luckily, my uncle and aunt looked after me like I was their own daughter. They'd never been able to have kids of their own, see. They were quite well off too, so I never wanted for anything." Hatsuko looked up at the ceiling. "I owe them everything, really."

"Funny. I always imagined you'd been born a prin-cess!"

"Well, my uncle always told me it'd be best not to tell people about the Yawatahama days. I'm sorry, though. It feels like I deceived you somehow." Hatsuko lowered her head in apology.

"Oh, not at all. Anyway, tell me about this fried rice."

"Right. The thing is, I don't actually remember it very well. Just the fact that I loved it. And that it was nothing like the kind you get at a Chinese restaurant."

"How was it different?" asked Koishi, raising her pen in anticipation.

"I can't really say," replied Hatsuko. She sank into thought for a moment. "I feel like it tasted a little . . . sour?"

"Sour, huh? I assume you don't mean it had gone bad or something."

"No, it wasn't that kind of sourness. More like a sort of tart aftertaste."

"Maybe she squeezed a lemon over it or something. What did it look like?"

"For some reason, I remember it being sort of . . . pink."

"Pink?" repeated Koishi, gaping in confusion. "Pink fried rice?"

"Look, you know how fried rice is normally sort of brown-looking? From the fried pork and everything. Well, the color was a lot brighter than that. I'd get home from school and there'd be this dish on my desk in the living room with a cloth laid over it. I just remember taking away the cloth and there being something pink underneath."

"So your mother was out when you got back from school?"

"Yeah. She had a part-time job and only got home late."

"And you'd microwave the rice and eat it on your own?" asked Koishi, her pen scratching away at her notebook.

"Yeah." Hatsuko smiled slightly. "While I did my homework."

"Do you know where this job of hers was?"

Hatsuko cocked her head. "It's all pretty blurry, but I think the company was called something like . . . Ehime Sumo."

"Ehime Sumo?" repeated Koishi, unable to help a chuckle. "You mean like the wrestlers? What sort of company calls itself *that*?"

"I might have it wrong," replied Hatsuko with a faint smile. "Maybe it's just because there was always sumo on the TV when I was eating it."

"Well, setting that to one side, is there anything you remember about the flavor? How was it different from regular fried rice?" Koishi turned to a fresh page in her notebook.

"Again, my memory is hazy, but I think it tasted sort of fishy. I reckon she used fish instead of meat. Yawatahama *was* a fishing town, after all."

"Fishy fried rice, huh?" said Koishi, setting down her pen and crossing her arms. "I can't quite imagine it."

"Sorry. Bit of a tricky one, isn't it?"

"Oh no, there's nothing to apologize for. Dad likes a challenge. But tell me—what made you want to eat this fried rice again all of a sudden?"

Hatsuko's features rearranged themselves into a troubled expression. Then, after a brief silence, she went on.

"Koishi, someone proposed to me last week."

"Wow!" said Koishi, clapping her hands with glee. "That's great news. Congratulations!"

"Thanks," murmured Hatsuko. But her eyes were downcast.

Koishi leaned forward. "Who's the lucky guy?"

"His name's Keita Kakuzawa."

"Mr. Kakuzawa, eh?"

"He's a managing director at Square Motors." A slight blush had come to Hatsuko's cheeks.

"No way." Koishi's eyes widened even further. "Let me guess: handsome, rich, heir to a fortune?"

Hatsuko gave a small nod. "He's set to inherit the whole company. We met after I appeared in one of their ads."

"Hatsuko, this is amazing news," said Koishi, unable to control her excitement.

"But I haven't given him my answer yet," replied Hatsuko, her gaze dropping to the table. "I mean, he's still in the dark about what my father did."

"What's that got to do with anything? I'm sure he'll understand."

A sad look came into Hatsuko's eyes. "The heir to one of Japan's biggest motor companies, and a penniless country bumpkin with a crook for a father. Does that sound like a good match to you?"

"But . . . but . . ." Koishi's voice grew quieter.

"I can't keep it under wraps forever. I think I have to just come out and tell him."

"But where does the fried rice come in?"

"He keeps saying he wants to try my cooking. I've been racking my brain over what to make him, but I think it has to be my mother's fried rice. That way, he'll get a sense of where I *really* come from." Hatsuko made a wry face.

"You know, Hatsuko, somehow, that's very like you."

"He knows I've been taking weekly cooking classes, so I bet he's expecting haute cuisine or a fancy kaiseki meal. He's in for a shock!"

"Well, this is all a little . . . complicated, but we'll do our best to make sure you get your happy ending." Koishi snapped her notebook shut, her expression serious.

"Thanks," said Hatsuko, pursing her lips as they rose to leave. "I just feel like until he's eaten that fried rice, he won't know the real me."

It was with a slightly heavy step that Koishi made her way back down the corridor, silently followed by Hatsuko. As they reentered the restaurant, Nagare folded up his newspaper and turned to Koishi. "Get all the details, then?"

"She certainly did," replied Hatsuko on her behalf.

"Judging from that frown, it's another tough one too," said Nagare, patting the glum-looking Koishi on the shoulder. She seemed at a loss for words, and again it was Hatsuko who eventually replied.

"Sorry for putting you to so much trouble."

"Don't you worry about a thing," said Nagare proudly. "The tricky ones are always the most rewarding."

Koishi seemed to have finally gathered herself, and now she turned to Hatsuko. "Will two weeks be okay?"

"Yes, I think that'll work. I wrote my email address on the form, so just drop me a line."

"Dad, you're going to have to go all out on this one," replied Koishi, glancing sideways at him.

"Oh, I will," said Nagare, smiling at Hatsuko.

"Thank you both so much." She bowed deeply, then slid open the door to the restaurant.

"Forgetting something?" asked Nagare, following her out with a black coat in his arms.

Hatsuko winced with embarrassment as she took it from him. "You don't know how many times I've done that."

"Glad to see you haven't lost your ditzy side," Koishi said, grinning.

Drowsy came scampering over. "Hello again, you," said Hatsuko, reaching down to pet him. "I'll be back soon, don't worry!"

"What does the rest of the day hold, then?" asked Nagare.

"I'm heading straight back to Tokyo," said Hatsuko, flagging down a passing taxi as she spoke. "I have a job later."

"You *are* a busy bee," said Koishi. "Just make sure you come to Kyoto every now and then for a bit of downtime, okay?"

"I wanted to stop by my uncle's grave too, but I just don't have time," said Hatsuko as she climbed into the taxi.

"Well, you look after yourself, okay?" called Nagare.

Hatsuko bowed as the taxi slowly pulled away. Nagare

and Koishi stood there waving until she'd disappeared from view, then stepped back inside.

"Something bothering you?" asked Nagare.

Koishi filled him in on the situation, then looked at him. "I'm not sure we should have agreed to help."

"Well, we have. All we can do now is give it our best shot," said Nagare decisively. "As for what she does with the result, that's up to Hatsuko. It's got nothing to do with you or me."

"I guess you're right," said Koishi, handing him her notebook with a look of relief. "Well, we'd better start investigating."

"Fried rice, eh?" said Nagare, slowly leafing through Koishi's handwritten notes. "Haven't had that in a while."

"Not just any fried rice. It's fishy. And pink," said Koishi, pointing over his shoulder at what she'd written. "Bit of a mystery, isn't it?"

"Hmm, Yawatahama . . ." said Nagare, tilting his head to one side. "I know they catch a lot of fish there, but I didn't think they'd go as far as using them in fried rice."

"About the color. What if she used finely chopped tuna, or some other fish with red flesh—wouldn't that look pink?"

"Not once she'd fried it," replied Nagare with a frown. "It'd turn darker."

"What if she sprinkled it with pickled ginger? You know, the pink type you see served with sushi."

"That wouldn't explain the fishy taste, though." Nagare closed the notebook. "Well, in any case, it looks like I'm off to Yawatahama."

"Another one of your field investigations, eh?" said Koishi, patting him on the back. "Well, make me proud!"

2

Hatsuko had always thought the term "lucky outfit" sounded a little trite, but she couldn't deny that some occasions called for a special effort. Today her coat was a striking red, with a deep crimson bag to match.

As her destination came into view, her pace slowed. She squatted to greet Drowsy, who came trotting over.

"Me again," she said, tickling his neck. "Told you I'd be back!"

"Watch out," called Koishi, sliding open the door of the restaurant. "He'll get fur on that lovely coat."

"Don't worry. Drowsy's a good boy. Aren't you?" Hatsuko got to her feet and adjusted the hem of her skirt.

"Dad's been so excited," said Koishi, placing a hand on Hatsuko's back and guiding her inside.

"I'm all nervous again!" Hatsuko placed a hand on

her chest, took a deep breath, then walked into the restaurant.

Nagare greeted her with a smile. "Ah. Good to see you."

"Hello again!" Hatsuko bowed slightly awkwardly, then removed her red coat.

"Cold in Kyoto, isn't it?" said Koishi.

"Yeah. Winter feels different down here, somehow."

"Well, everything's ready," said Nagare as he poured her a cup of tea. "Just say the word."

"Thank you," said Hatsuko, flexing her shoulders up and down. "I just need a moment to gather myself."

Koishi studied her for a moment, then asked, "Can I get you some sake?"

"Let's save the drinking for afterward," said Nagare. "Hatsuko needs to feel like she's a kid again."

"Okay, I'm ready." Hatsuko had steadied her breathing and now sat up straight in her chair. "Let's do this."

"I'll bring it through in exactly three minutes," said Nagare, hurrying off to the kitchen.

Hatsuko closed her eyes and pursed her lips. Perhaps it was the effect of the dry winter air that filled the restaurant, but she could clearly make out every little noise that came from the kitchen. There was a distinctive beep, followed by the sound of a microwave oven being opened and closed. Soon afterward, Nagare came bustling back in with an aluminum tray, on top of which was the plate of fried rice.

"Heated up in the microwave, just like when you were a kid. Watch out—it's hot." Nagare set the round white plate down in front of her, followed by a spoon. The cling film covering the dish was clouded with steam, so that she could only vaguely discern what lay beneath.

"Can I take the cling film off?" asked Hatsuko, glancing up at Nagare.

He nodded decisively. "Please. That's all part of it."

Hatsuko smiled at him, then peeled away the film. A cloud of steam billowed up from the plate.

"Well, enjoy!" Nagare signaled to Koishi with his eyes, and the two of them retreated to the kitchen.

Hatsuko pressed her palms together over the plate and prepared to tuck in. Her nose twitched at the faint fragrance of the steam rising from the plate. Using the spoon, she scooped a mouthful of rice from the top of the mound, slowly brought it to her mouth, closed her eyes, and chewed. After a few seconds, she nodded deeply.

"Yes. This is it."

Then, as if suddenly possessed by some mysterious force, she began frantically spooning the fried rice into her mouth.

When the plate was just over half empty, she stopped to murmur a single word: "Amazing."

"Well?" asked Nagare, appearing at her side with an Arita-ware teapot. "Does it taste the same?"

"Absolutely," replied Hatsuko, still speaking in a murmur.

"Really? Wonderful," said Nagare as he refilled her cup. "I made plenty, so eat as much as you like, all right?"

"But Nagare, this—"

"Just enjoy it for now," said Nagare, cutting her off. "We can talk about it when you're done." He made his way back into the kitchen.

Hatsuko continued eating, savoring the taste more deliberately now. Spoonful by spoonful, she carefully transported the rice to her mouth. As she did so, her childhood memories began to return to her, clearer than ever before.

Crying all the way home from school after the other children had teased her about her height. Unlocking the front door, then almost fainting at the sight of an enormous spider. Being left home alone during a rainstorm and scrabbling about desperately for buckets when the roof began to leak. And hating, more than anything else, those silly red dresses she was always being made to wear.

It wasn't all bad, though. There was the time they'd all gone to Suwazaki together and seen the most wonderful sunset. Or that picnic underneath the cherry blossoms on the banks of the Kiki River.

For a long time, she'd buried these memories somewhere deep inside her. Now they all came rushing back at once. Before she knew it, the plate in front of her was empty.

"Could I have some more, please?" she called.

Nagare appeared from the kitchen, smiling from ear to ear. "Of course."

Hatsuko beamed back at him. "I feel like I could eat it forever."

"That's music to my ears," said Nagare. He placed her empty plate on his tray and hurried back to the kitchen.

Hatsuko remembered an evening when, desperate for seconds, she'd scoured the kitchen for any other food she could find. The fridge, the cupboards, even—with the help of a footstool—the top shelf that was normally out of reach. But she'd found nothing. Still ravenous, she'd resorted to drinking glass after glass of water, in an attempt to at least fill her belly with *something*.

Nagare set the replenished plate of fried rice down in front of her. "I've given you a half portion this time, but just let me know if it's not enough."

"Thank you," said Hatsuko, already digging her spoon into the rice. "This looks like plenty."

"Makes me so glad to see you tucking in like that," said Nagare, smiling. "Bringing back plenty of memories, is it?"

"It must be years since I ate this much in one go. It's bizarre. My spoon just won't stop moving."

"Normally it's only kids who get to eat like that. Completely absorbed in their food. Once we grow up, all we do is worry about healthy eating and diets and what have you." Nagare's eyes narrowed as he smiled. "Maybe you've rediscovered your inner child."

"You know," said Hatsuko once she had made a significant dent in the mound of rice, "I think it's about time you told me how on earth you managed to pull this off."

"All right. Shall I get us a drink?" asked Nagare, miming a sip from a sake cup.

"Funny you should say that, Dad," said Koishi, appearing from the kitchen with a lacquered tray, on which she'd placed a large Shigaraki-ware sake bottle and three matching cups. "I planned ahead."

"The one area where your intuition really shines," said Nagare, sitting down opposite Hatsuko.

"I'm just glad you managed to get the fried rice right. It's a weight off my shoulders too," said Koishi, raising her sake cup. Nagare and Hatsuko followed her lead.

"So," said Nagare once he'd drained his cup. "I took a little trip to Yawatahama."

"You went all that way?" Hatsuko bowed her head. "Thank you."

"Unfortunately, I couldn't find anyone who knew Mr.

Shirasaki, but I did find out about that company your mother did part-time work for. They went out of business a while back, but the name of the company was Aihachi Foods. They were the first in the country to sell fish sausages. That's when it hit me. The pink ingredient in your fried rice: it had to be these." Nagare produced a packet of fish sausages from a plastic bag at his side. "You must have noticed them in the rice?"

"Oh yes," said Hatsuko. "You know, I think I remember seeing something like that in our fridge."

"I picked these up in Yawatahama. A local butcher told me this brand was the closest you could get to the type Aihachi Foods used to make." Nagare set the sausages to one side, then produced another packet from his bag. "Now, this was the *other* reason for that pink color."

"What's that?" asked Hatsuko.

"A Yawatahama specialty. Kamaboko flakes. Just like bonito flakes, except made from kamaboko fish cake instead of tuna. They were invented back before people had fridges, as a way of making kamaboko last longer. Normally you'd sprinkle them over things like chirashi-zushi, but your mother decided they'd be a good addition to her fried rice. They make a pretty decent drinking snack too, by the way." Nagare opened the packet and retrieved a handful of the flakes, which he began to nibble on.

"So it wasn't just the fish sausage, then," said Hatsuko, also sampling the flakes.

"That's right," said Koishi, grabbing a handful for herself. "Given what they're both made from, it's no wonder you remembered the fried rice having a fishy flavor."

"As for the all-important seasoning," continued Nagare, "I imagine she used a mix of shredded shio-kombu and sour plum. That's where that tart aftertaste you mentioned came from. Then I realized: sour plum is pink too. It all fits the color scheme, see?" He showed her a can of the shredded kelp and sour plum mix. Hatsuko gave a deep, appreciative nod.

"As for the rice, I think any type would work. Now, all your ingredients are in here"—he handed her a paper bag—"and I've written out the recipe too, so you should be all set. This fiancé of yours will be begging for seconds."

"Well," said Hatsuko, getting to her feet, "thank you for everything."

Koishi jumped up from her chair. "Leaving so soon? You can always stay for dinner, you know."

"Sorry. I have work to get back to," replied Hatsuko as she gathered her things. "And I'm going to stop by my uncle's grave and pay my respects on the way."

"Well, you know where to come if you ever fancy a bite to eat," said Nagare.

"I can't wait. That reminds me—I completely forgot to pay last time." Hatsuko extracted a red patent-leather wallet from her bag. "How much do I owe you for everything?"

"We leave the food-finding fee up to the client," said Koishi, handing her a slip of paper. "Just transfer however much you feel it was worth to this account."

"Got it," replied Hatsuko as she folded the slip up and tucked it into her wallet. "I promise you won't be disappointed."

As she stepped outside, Drowsy the cat strolled over and began mewing at her feet.

"Thanks for having me, Drowsy!" said Hatsuko, picking him up and stroking him affectionately. "I'll be back soon, I promise."

"Hey, you," said Nagare, poking the cat in the belly. "You'll get fur all over her expensive coat."

Hatsuko set Drowsy back down, then turned to Nagare and Koishi and bowed. "I really appreciate this, you two."

"We should have called you a taxi," said Koishi, standing on her tiptoes and glancing up and down Shomen-dori.

"Don't worry," said Hatsuko, facing west down the street. "I'm sure I'll find one on Karasuma-dori."

"You take care!" called Nagare. Hatsuko bobbed her head, then strode off down the street.

"You can tell she's a model, can't you?" said Nagare to Koishi with a grin. "Just look at that strut."

"Hatsuko!" called Koishi. Hatsuko stopped and turned. Koishi cupped her hands around her mouth and yelled: "Go get him, okay?"

Hatsuko smiled and nodded in reply. Then, with another wave, she set off once more.

Nagare and Koishi waited for her to disappear from sight, then went back inside.

"I hope it all goes okay," said Koishi as they cleared the dishes.

"Hope what goes okay?"

"Isn't it obvious?" asked Koishi, running a cloth across the table. "Her engagement to Mr. Kakuzawa!"

"Does it really matter either way?" said Nagare. He gave the sake bottle a shake to confirm it was empty. "It's all in the hands of the gods now."

Koishi folded her arms. "With a figure like that, she'd look amazing in a Western wedding dress."

"Whereas you'll definitely be in a kimono," said Nagare, settling at the counter with his newspaper. "Your hair all done up. Nice and traditional."

"I'd say the bigger question, in this hypothetical situation of yours, is who I'm marrying," said Koishi, sitting down next to him.

"Well," Nagare said with a smile, "how about we head

over to Hiroshi's for sushi tonight? We haven't been there for a while."

Koishi's eyes seemed to twinkle. "Really?"

"We do need to find you a nice guy before too long," said Nagare, slipping off his shoes as he stepped up into the tatami-floored living room and sat by the altar. "Kikuko will be getting worried!"

Koishi followed him into the room. "Oh, I don't know about that. She's probably more concerned about whether you'd be able to fend for yourself."

Nagare lit a stick of incense, carefully positioned it in front of the altar, then addressed himself to the photo of Kikuko.

"Thanks for always looking out for us—and Hatsuko too."

Chapter 5

Ramen

1

Kyoto is no place for a summer holiday. That was what Katsuji Onodera was always telling people—and yet here he was, getting off a train at Kyoto station on a sultry midsummer day. He had to laugh.

More than three decades had passed since his four years here as a student. He had plenty of fond memories from those days, but the city's sweltering summers and bitter winters were not among them. In particular, he had loathed the summers, when the humid air seemed to cling to your body and refuse to let go.

From the train, Kyoto seemed just as he remembered it, and at the same time seemed to have changed beyond recognition. Clearly, the city was still capable of casting its mysterious spell on him.

He made his way out of the station's Hachijo exit and climbed into a taxi. As they reached the other side of the gently curving bridge that spanned the railway tracks, he glimpsed a long line that had formed outside a famous ramen restaurant. These days, it was one of the biggest chains in the country. You could even buy their brand of instant ramen in convenience stores. Remembering the taste of their noodles, which he still ate whenever he missed Kyoto, Katsuji turned in his seat and gazed at the restaurant through the rear window.

The taxi made its way north up Karasuma-dori. Just as Higashi Honganji temple came into view on the left, the driver turned right onto Shomen-dori.

"Round here somewhere, is it?" asked the driver, slowing and glancing up and down the street.

"You can let me out here. I'll walk the rest of the way."

Katsuji climbed out of the taxi, clutching his black holdall to his chest.

"Right," he murmured to himself. "If this is Shomen-dori . . . and Higashi Honganji is that way . . . Ah, here we go." He looked up at a two-story, mortar-walled building, then down at the map in his hand.

No sign, and no curtain over the entrance like other restaurants had. Anyone would assume it was a private residence. *Could this really be the place?* he wondered. Katsuji went ahead and slid the aluminum door open, before timidly venturing inside.

Spotting a woman who appeared to work there, he asked, "Is this the . . . Kamogawa Diner, by any chance?"

"It is. Here for a meal?"

"If you wouldn't mind. Though I'm really here for the, erm, detective service." Katsuji presented his business card.

"Well then, take a seat. I'm in charge of the agency." She bobbed her head in his direction. "Koishi Kamogawa. As for the restaurant—that's my dad's jurisdiction."

Katsuji seemed momentarily flustered by the fact that this young, unassuming woman was, in fact, the head of a detective agency.

"Do we have a customer, Koishi?" said a man in chef's whites, striding out of the kitchen.

"He's here for the detective service," said Koishi, turning to face him. "But he'd like a bite to eat too."

"Pleased to meet you, Mr. . . . Onodera," said Nagare, glancing at the business card Katsuji handed him. "We serve first-time customers a set menu. Will that be all right?"

"That would be perfect," replied Katsuji, his face creasing into a relieved smile.

"I'll just get that ready for you, then. Give me a moment!" Nagare made his way back into the kitchen.

Settling at a table, Katsuji glanced around the restaurant

properly for the first time. There was only one other customer—an elderly, kimono-clad lady at the rearmost table who had just finished sipping on her matcha tea. Her elegant appearance was so at odds with the restaurant's homely interior that for a moment, he simply stared at her.

"Have you come far?" she asked, catching his gaze.

"Tokyo."

"Are people my age a rare sight there, or something?" There was an edge to the woman's voice.

"Sorry, I . . . couldn't help admiring your kimono." Katsuji gave an apologetic bow. "People in Tokyo barely know how to wear them anymore."

"Tae is a rare breed even by Kyoto standards, you know," said Koishi, pouring the woman some more tea. "Wonderful posture, never breaks a sweat even on a hot day like this—and dresses up in a kimono whenever she eats out. She's basically my idol!"

"Flattery will get you everywhere," said Tae, giving Koishi a sidelong glance as she reached for the Karatsu-ware teacup in front of her.

"Sorry, but I'm a little thirsty," said Katsuji, dabbing at his neck with a handkerchief. "Could I get a beer?"

"We only have the large bottles."

"That'll be fine."

Koishi popped the cap on the bottle, filled a small glass, and set them both on his table.

"I lived here as a student," said Katsuji, smiling at Tae after he'd drained the glass. "Kyoto really *is* the place to wear a kimono, isn't it?"

"Where did you study?"

"Rakushikan University."

"Well, I'm sure it was a very amusing time for you," said Tae a little coldly.

"Oh yes," said Katsuji, topping up his glass so vigorously that foam spilled onto the table.

"Sounds like there's something you want to get off your chest, Tae?" said Koishi, refilling her tea with an earthenware Mashiko teapot.

"I'm sure things are different *these* days, but a few decades ago studying at Rakushikan was synonymous with having rather a wild time of it. It was common knowledge that anyone who actually cared about their studies went to Kyonan University. Rakushikan was for messing around."

Katsuji smiled faintly as he finished his second glass of beer.

"Oh, I don't know about that," said Nagare, setting a black lacquered tray down in front of Katsuji. "All sorts of interesting people have come out of that place."

"Thanks for the support." Katsuji grinned, emptying the last of the bottle into his glass.

"Not to mention various celebrities," continued Nagare, arranging a pair of Rikyu chopsticks and a blue-and-white china plate on the tray. "And plenty of big shots in the business world."

"Lots of my friends too," Koishi chimed in.

"Well, precisely," said Tae sharply. "I imagine *those* are the types of students who like to stay up all night making a racket."

"Guilty as charged," said Katsuji, scratching his head sheepishly.

Nagare set a large glass platter down, on which various smaller dishes were arranged. "I hope this'll be to your liking."

"Ah," said Katsuji, his eyes lighting up as he leaned forward to inspect the array of food before him.

"Everything on this platter is hamo eel or ayu sweet-fish: two essential parts of Kyoto summer cuisine," explained Nagare. "Starting from the top left: miniature hamo sushi rolls. One teriyaki-style, and one shirayaki—without any seasoning, that is. Next to that, in the small bowl, is shredded hamo eel skin, pickled and served with okra. On top of the bamboo grass leaf are two little ayu, caught in the Katsura River—salted and grilled. In the glass sake cup is a delicacy known as uruka—basically the salted entrails and roe of the ayu. Similar to shiokara, if you've had that. The deep-fried dish in the middle on the right is ayu fry. They're sprinkled with sansho pepper salt, so you can enjoy them as they are. Bottom right, on the perilla leaf, is hamo no otoshi: boiled slices of the eel, served with pickled plum paste and myoga ginger. Bottom left, meanwhile, is hamo no hasamiyaki, which is seasoned with white miso and fried between slices of Yamashina eggplant." Nagare bowed in conclusion. "Please, enjoy at your leisure."

"Fancy another one of these?" asked Koishi, picking up the empty beer bottle. "Or can I get you some sake?"

"Oh, I can't be drinking plain old beer with a meal like this. Sake would be perfect." Katsuji licked his lips at the sight in front of him.

"I just got a new one in that ought to be a good match," said Nagare. "From a brewery up in Fukushima. I'll fetch it for you." He bustled off to the kitchen.

"Well, I'm off," said Tae. "Enjoy the meal." She bowed slightly and made her way out of the restaurant. Katsuji rose from his chair and bowed in return.

Once he'd watched her depart, he picked up his chopsticks and reached for the uruka. He positioned a small dab of the salted entrails on his chopsticks and inserted it into his mouth. Then he closed his eyes, as if in rapture.

"Here you go," said Nagare, appearing with a glass

tumbler of sake on a tray. "Ninki, it's called. They only sell it in the summer. It's a junmai ginjo, chilled to around fifty degrees. Anyway, I'll leave you to it. Just let me know when you're ready for the soup, and I'll bring that through." Nagare slipped the silver tray under his arm and retreated to the kitchen.

The Edo Kiriko cut-glass tumbler was full to the brim with sake. Katsuji raised it to his mouth, took a long sip, and sighed contentedly. It tasted sublime.

Next he marveled at the hasamiyaki dish, in which the hamo eel was combined with the delicate sweetness of white miso. Hamo had been way out of his budget as a student. Even now that he could afford it whenever he was in town, it always seemed to taste the same. The masters of various high-end restaurants had all insisted to him that hamo was the highlight of the Kyoto summer, but he'd never really been convinced. Now, as he placed the eel on his tongue, he finally understood.

The ayu, too, tasted extraordinary. Not just the grilled salted ones—those were always going to be delicious— but the tiny deep-fried ones, each smaller than his little finger, also had a pleasing bitterness, one that brought to mind the mountain streams where they were caught, and that combined with the sansho pepper to leave a piquant aftertaste on the tongue.

As the founder of a successful medium-size company, Katsuji had eaten at his fair share of upscale restaurants in Tokyo, but none of them could hold a candle to what Kyoto had to offer. This wasn't even some famous Gion restaurant, either: he was sitting in the "diner" attached to a detective agency, of all places.

"All okay?" asked Nagare, appearing at his side.

"No beating the food in Kyoto, is there? I've never had anything like this in Tokyo."

Nagare eyed his near-empty tumbler. "Can I top you up?"

"I'm tempted to say yes, but I don't want to get too distracted from the task at hand."

"In that case, I'll bring that soup through. Shall I fetch you some of today's rice too? It's cooked with ayu."

"Oh, please!"

As Nagare made his way back to the kitchen, Katsuji surveyed the food that remained in front of him, then had another sip of his sake. He let it trickle slowly down his throat. Then he remembered why he'd come here in the first place, and all of a sudden the alcohol tasted slightly bitter.

"Here's the soup. Nothing new, but if you're going to have broth in summer, it has to be botan-hamo: lightly boiled hamo eel, named for the way it's cut into the shape of a peony to remove the bones. As for this ayu rice, the only ingredient is in the name. The fish are deboned, so all you need to do is sprinkle some of these chopped mitsuba leaves on top. The pickles on the side are eggplant and myoga ginger. Now, you tuck in, and I'll bring you a cup of hojicha."

As soon as Nagare had disappeared, Katsuji cupped the bowl of soup in his hands and raised it to his lips.

The faint fragrance of kombu drifted up from the bowl. He tried a mouthful and felt the tender hamo melt on his tongue. The delicate flavor of the soy-infused broth seemed to seep into his entire body. Trying to restrain his excitement, Katsuji set the broth down and reached instead for the ayu rice that had been generously heaped in a Koimari bowl. As he chewed, he noticed the slight bitterness of the ayu fusing harmoniously with the sweetness of the rice. It was exquisite.

Nagare returned with an earthenware Shigaraki teapot. "You know, on a hot day like this, a cup of hot hojicha is actually just what you need."

"That was an incredible meal, really," said Katsuji, bringing his palms together in a gesture of gratitude. "I've tried plenty of Kyoto cuisine in my time, but I feel like this was the real deal. I hope you don't mind me saying that I didn't expect to find it here, of all places."

"Well, I don't know if it really qualifies as Kyoto cuisine," said Nagare as he cleared the dishes and wiped the table down. "I just make whatever I feel like, you see."

"When I was a student, our professor used to take us out for meals at fancy restaurants in Gion every now and then. But none of the food we ate has really stayed with me—in fact, I barely remember it."

"You appreciate things differently when you're older, don't you? Food is never just about flavor. It's something we *feel*—and in different ways, depending on where we are in life."

Katsuji nodded in silent agreement.

"Koishi's waiting in the office. Shall I show you through?"

"Lead the way," said Katsuji. He finished his tea and got to his feet.

As he followed Nagare down the long, narrow corridor that led to the rear of the restaurant, he found himself gazing, spellbound, at the hundreds of photos lining its walls.

"Mostly just experiments of mine," explained Nagare over his shoulder.

In the photos, French-style dishes rubbed shoulders with huge hot-pot cauldrons; spreads of osechi cuisine were accompanied by enormous banquet platters. He was so preoccupied by them that he barely noticed they had reached the end of the corridor.

"Please," said Nagare. He opened the door to reveal Koishi, perched expectantly on a sofa.

"Right, then," said Koishi, once Katsuji had taken a seat opposite her. She handed him a clipboard. "Could you jot your details down here for me?"

Katsuji blitzed his way through the form like one might a hotel register. When he returned it to Koishi, she began reading aloud.

"Katsushi Onodera. Address in Meguro, Tokyo—"

"Katsu*ji*. It's Katsuji Onodera."

"Oops, sorry. Right, then. Occupation . . . managing director of Theater Print Limited. Is that a printing company?"

"Yes. I founded it not long after graduating from Rakushikan, when I came back to Tokyo. It's a pretty modest operation, really."

"Let me guess: business cards, New Year's cards—that kind of thing?"

"We do those, yes, but our specialty is actually CD jackets. I don't mean to brag, but our share of the Japanese market stands at over fifty percent. Though, mind you, CDs themselves seem to be something of a dying breed these days." The smile on Katsuji's face suggested a peculiar blend of pride and self-deprecation.

"Dad's a big fan of old enka songs, you know."

"Enka, eh? Our share of that particular market stands at over eighty percent."

"Really? Dad'll love that. Now, back to the matter at hand: What is this dish you'd like us to re-create?"

Koishi leaned forward. "I'm a little embarrassed to tell you this, but it's the ramen from a food stall. You know, one of those yatai places that pop up at nighttime by the river. Though actually, the owner insisted on calling it 'Chinese noodles' instead of ramen."

"And where was this yatai?" asked Koishi. Her notebook was open, her pen raised in anticipation.

"See, right after I started at Rakushikan, I joined the drama club. Me and two other guys from my year—Kunisue and Yasaka, their names were—started our own three-man troupe. The Hamsters, we called ourselves. I think we only turned up to about half our assigned lectures. But every day at sundown, regardless of whether we'd shown up on campus that day, we'd meet underneath Kitaoji Bridge and rehearse. And that was where the yatai stall was."

"A yatai by the Kitaoji Bridge. What was the name?"

"I don't think it had one."

"Right. And this would have been . . . what year?" Koishi asked.

"This was around 1975. I'm pretty sure the yatai was still there when I graduated in '79."

Koishi jotted these details down in her notebook. "Which side of the bridge was it?"

"The opposite side from Mount Hiei. In other words—" Katsuji broke off as he tried to visualize the area.

"The west side," said Koishi with assurance.

"In my third year, the trams stopped running over Kitaoji Bridge," said Katsuji, his eyes growing distant. "The times were changing, I guess."

"Tell me about this ramen, then."

"Would you know what I meant if I said it tasted like, well, yatai ramen? It wasn't all oily, like a lot of ramen is these days, but it wasn't exactly light on the stomach, either. It really filled you up."

"But with yatai-style ramen, the soup is usually pretty thick, isn't it?" said Koishi, readying her pen again.

"See, that's just it. I mean, sure, it was quite cloudy, and rich enough in flavor, but it wasn't like the type you see everywhere now, with a thick layer of oil floating on the surface. It was—how can I put this . . . milder, somehow."

"You're making me want to try it! By the time I went to university, those yatai places had almost all shut down."

"They were all over the city in my day. You know the Masugata shopping arcade in Demachi? There must have been four ramen stalls there alone."

"So, what made you want to eat this ramen again, after all these years?" Koishi turned to a fresh page in her notebook.

"My son was supposed to take over the family business. Now, all of a sudden, he's telling me it's not for him. Says he wants to become a stage actor instead." Katsuji frowned. "How's he going to make a living out of that?"

"Why shouldn't he follow his dream? He's taking after his old man, after all."

"But dreams are only ever just that—dreams. Reality has a habit of biting, you know."

"What does all this have to do with the ramen, then?"

"See, back then, I had dreams of my own," replied Katsuji, his eyes fixed on the low table in front of him. "And in a sense, the ramen from that yatai was what fueled them. My company isn't such a big deal, and I don't want to force my son into doing something he'd rather not. I want him to follow his heart. It's just . . . I worry about his future, you see. Just like I used to worry about my own future when I was his age." Katsuji had begun to gaze off into space.

"Dreams versus reality, eh? That's adulthood for you."

"Especially back then, if you were a man, you had to

think about how you were going to provide for your family. Now, if that's *all* you think about, life can be a little dull—but on the other hand, if you run around chasing your dreams willy-nilly, you're sure to come a cropper eventually. At the end of the day, you have to choose a life that'll put food on the table. And that usually means making some kind of compromise."

"Meanwhile, your son wants to chase his dream."

"The kid's chances of actually making it are one in ten thousand."

"That's better than zero, though, isn't it?" said Koishi.

Katsuji looked steadily at her. "You know, I've been telling my son no, but there's a part of me, deep inside, that wants to tell him yes. And for some reason, whenever I try to put my finger on where that urge comes from, I find myself thinking of the ramen from that yatai."

"And if you could just eat it one more time, you'd feel ready to talk things over with your son?" asked Koishi, returning his gaze.

"Oh, I don't know if it'll come to that. For now, I just want to work out how I really feel about it all. That's all."

"Right, then," said Koishi, snapping her notebook shut. "Well, I guess the most important thing right now is that we track down this ramen and serve it up to you. And all we have to go on is the location, eh? Don't worry, Dad'll know what to do. He always does."

"Thank you very much," said Katsuji, bowing in her direction.

As they reentered the restaurant, Nagare looked up from his newspaper.

"Good interview?"

"Oh yes. I got all the details. It's ramen from a yatai stall, Dad. You've got your work cut out for you!" said Koishi, clapping him on the shoulder.

Nagare got to his feet and looked at Katsuji. "Yatai ramen, eh? That brings back a few memories. This city used to be full of those places."

"I imagine it won't be easy now that they're all gone," said Katsuji, the corner of his mouth lifting in a painful smile.

Nagare bowed slightly. "Don't worry. I'll search high and low."

"Can I pay for the meal?" asked Katsuji, slipping a long wallet from his suit pocket.

"We'll settle up next time—including our fee for finding that ramen," Koishi replied, smiling.

"All right, then. And when should I come back?" Katsuji looked expectantly at them.

"Give us two weeks or so. We can talk more over the

phone if needed. I'll reach you on your mobile, if that's all right?" asked Nagare, eyeing Katsuji's business card.

"Thank you, that sounds perfect," said Katsuji, picking up his holdall and making his way outside.

"Any plans for the rest of the day?" asked Nagare.

"It's been a while since I was last in town. I thought I'd stop by a few old haunts." Katsuji squinted up at the blue summer sky.

"Take care in this heat, okay?" said Koishi.

As they talked, Drowsy the cat came skipping over.

"Hey, you," said Nagare, glaring as he bent down to collect the cat. "Don't even think about going inside."

Katsuji made his way down Shomen-dori, heading east. Nagare and Koishi watched him go, then turned back inside.

Nagare sank into one of the counter seats and began leafing through Koishi's notebook. "The west side of Kitaoji Bridge, eh? Can't say I remember any ramen stalls around there."

Koishi glanced up from the table she was wiping. "He said the owner actually called it 'Chinese noodles.'"

"Hmm. And he runs a printing company? Theater Print Limited. Interesting." Nagare tucked Katsuji's business card into the notebook. "Well, looks like I have a bit of legwork to do. I'll pop over that way tomorrow."

"Kitaoji Bridge—that's near the botanical garden. Remember that cherry-blossom picnic we did there in the spring, along the Nakaragi Path?"

"That gives me an idea. There's an old shopping arcade on that side of the bridge. Maybe someone there will know something."

Nagare closed the notebook.

2

The trees lining Shomen-dori were abuzz with cicadas. When Katsuji had lived in Kyoto, he'd been used to the sight of the brown-winged type, but those were probably outnumbered by the larger, green-winged variant these days. After all, the larger ones fared much better during the hot summers that were becoming so common. As he waited for the signal to change, Katsuji frowned and dabbed the sweat from his neck with his handkerchief.

He crossed Karasuma-dori, making his way east until he found himself standing in front of his destination. After a brief pause to catch his breath, he slid open the door to the Kamogawa Diner.

"Ah," said Nagare, coming over to the entrance. A small towel was draped around his neck. "Good to see you again."

"What is . . . that?" asked Katsuji, his eyes widening at the sight of an old wooden bench. He didn't remember seeing anything like it during his last visit.

"Ah, that thing . . . Dad said it was almost as hard to track down as the ramen itself!" commented Koishi with a smile.

The bench was flaking red paint, its planks badly worn, and the name and red logo of a major beverage company could be faintly discerned.

"Ah, now I remember. There was a bench just like this at the yatai. Wow, you really have pulled out all the stops." Katsuji stroked the back of the bench, a dreamy, nostalgic look in his eyes.

"It's not *just* for your benefit," said Koishi in a low, mischievous voice. "Dad said he could put it outside for smokers to use. Tae keeps telling him to make this place no-smoking."

"I don't know what the world's coming to," said Nagare. "Anyway, take a seat."

Katsuji did as instructed, slowly lowering himself onto the bench.

"You know, when we first started rehearsing under that bridge, the man who ran the yatai wasn't too happy about it. Kept shouting at us to keep it down."

Koishi and Nagare stood on either side of the bench while Katsuji recounted his memories.

"We decided to eat his ramen as our way of paying for the use of the space. I think it was Kunisue's idea. He figured that if we became the guy's customers, he couldn't keep yelling at us. Always had a good head for that kind of thing, did Kunisue."

"And once you tried it, you were hooked?" asked Nagare.

"No, actually. I didn't think it was anything special. I knew plenty of other places where you could get ramen that was just as good, if not better."

"The ramen scene in Kyoto has always been pretty competitive," said Nagare.

"Eating there was more like an obligation—like Kunisue said, a way of paying for the space. We rehearsed almost every day, but only splurged on the ramen every three days or so. The funny thing is, the more I ate it, the more I came to enjoy it. I suppose I got used to the taste or something. At some point, I started actively looking forward to it." Katsuji paused, a faint smile coming to his lips.

"Here," said Koishi, handing him a slightly battered plastic cup of chilled water.

"Ah, yes. The cups were just like this!" exclaimed Katsuji, before downing the water in one go.

"It'll just be a minute," said Nagare, heading for the kitchen.

"This is giving me goose bumps," said Katsuji, cracking his knuckles. "Feels like I've gone back in time."

Koishi grinned as she refilled his cup. "I told Dad we should put on some throwback tunes for good measure—but he was having none of it."

Katsuji chuckled and set the cup on the bench. His nostrils began to twitch as the fragrance of ramen broth drifted from the kitchen.

"Something smells good."

"Yeah. It's making me hungry too!" said Koishi, putting a hand to her stomach.

They fell silent. From the kitchen came the sound of the noodles being drained, followed by the drumlike rhythm of Nagare's approaching footsteps.

"Here we are," he said, arriving with his silver tray. On it, perched on a white plastic saucer with a pair of disposable chopsticks and a spoon, was the bowl of ramen.

"My word!" said Katsuji, taking the saucer before cupping the small bowl in his left hand. "It's exactly the same!"

"I'll leave the pepper here," said Nagare, setting a large shaker by the cup on the bench. "Enjoy." He disappeared back into the kitchen, followed by Koishi.

With the bowl still in his left hand, Katsuji gave the ramen a good sprinkle of white pepper. Returning the shaker to the bench, he reached for the disposable wooden chopsticks, then broke them apart with his teeth. Then, using the flat-bottomed spoon, he raised a mouthful of the broth to his nose, gave it a good sniff, then carefully slurped it down.

He detected a faint hint of tonkotsu in the broth, but the base was definitely chicken rather than pig bones. The broth wasn't quite transparent, but it was a great deal clearer than the turbid liquid that usually accompanied ramen these days. It seemed quite possible there was some kind of fish stock in there too. A garlicky, gingery aroma rose from the bowl.

The noodles were the thin, straight type, and cooked slightly on the firm side. On top of them lay two slices of roast pork and another two of kamaboko fish cake. These were accompanied by bean sprouts, pickled bamboo shoots, and negi onion. He tried one of the slices of roast pork—leg meat, by the looks of it. It was delicious. To Katsuji it all tasted like the distant past, but also, strangely, like something very close to him now.

He had done his homework before coming to the restaurant, reading books about ramen and even visiting a few well-known establishments. Now he tried to apply his newfound knowledge to an analysis of the ramen in front of him, only to realize, almost immediately, that such an approach was futile. Instead, he let his mind turn blank and simply ate. Slurping the noodles, spooning down the broth, and chewing away at the toppings: he simply concentrated on repeating these three actions, over and over.

Instead of flavor-analysis charts, long-forgotten memories began racing through his mind. As the broth trickled down his throat, he remembered lines from plays; as he chewed the noodles, laughter seemed to echo in his ears. In the hand gripping the bowl, he could almost feel the many hours during which they'd excitedly discussed their dreams. Tears began to well in Katsuji's eyes.

"Taste about right, then?" asked Nagare from behind the bench.

Katsuji turned around, the bowl in his hand now empty. "Oh yes."

"That's good to hear," said Nagare, nodding and smiling.

"Unless my memory's mistaken, the flavor was identical. That was the exact bowl of noodles I ate all those years ago. How on earth did you . . . ?"

"Well, the yatai is long gone, of course. But I found someone who remembered it very well." Nagare produced a sepia-toned photo. It showed a smallish man, grinning bashfully as he set up a yatai stall by a bridge.

Katsuji leaned in and began poring over the photo's every detail. "Yes, that's the place. And that's him!"

"There's a famous restaurant just to the northwest of Kitaoji Bridge—Grill Hasegawa. Mr. Hasegawa, the owner, remembered the yatai well. It turns out it was run by a gentleman named Seiji Yasumoto."

"Mr. Yasumoto, eh?" said Katsuji, gazing off into space. "You know, I don't think we ever caught his name."

"He used to borrow water and electricity from Mr. Hasegawa. Even after he closed his yatai, the two of them stayed in touch. Mr. Yasumoto ended up opening a ramen restaurant on Ryogaemachi-dori—Yasu-san, it was called. Mr. Hasegawa used to turn up there every now and then for a bowl of noodles. Unfortunately, Mr. Yasumoto passed away ten years ago from illness. He didn't have any family to pass the restaurant on to, so the place simply went out of business. And that was where the trail seemed to end." Nagare showed him a photo of Mr. Yasumoto's yatai in its heyday.

Katsuji glanced at the photograph, then adopted a doubtful expression. "Then how did you . . . make this?"

"There's always another connection," said Nagare, sitting down on one of the chairs opposite Katsuji's bench. "You just have to know where to look."

"Hot or iced tea?" asked Koishi, setting a teacup on the bench.

"Hot, please."

Koishi filled his cup with hojicha from her Mashiko teapot. He took a sip and waited for Nagare to go on.

"Mr. Hasegawa told me that Mr. Yasumoto's ashes had

been interred at Saihoji temple, not far from his restaurant. So I thought I'd go and pay my respects. I was at loose ends, see, and all I could think of was asking the man himself." It was hard to tell from Nagare's expression whether he was joking or serious.

"When I got there, I saw from the wooden dedication tablets by the grave that someone else had been visiting every month, on the day on which Mr. Yasumoto had passed away. The name written on the tablets was Daisuke Kanehara. I couldn't shake the feeling that I'd heard it before somewhere." Nagare paused to sip his tea.

"Daisuke Kanehara?" asked Katsuji, tilting his head to one side. "Never heard of him."

"Tell me, are you familiar with the ramen chain Shinsen Kyoichi?

"Of course. When I was a student, it was a small, one-shop operation. These days it's a huge company. They even have their own brand of instant noodles, don't they? I pick up a pack in Tokyo whenever I fancy a trip down memory lane."

"Well, Mr. Kanehara is the company's president. I went and saw him. He's a very busy man, but when I mentioned Mr. Yasumoto's name, he agreed to meet right away." Nagare took another sip of his tea. Katsuji leaned forward, grasping his own empty teacup as he waited eagerly for Nagare to continue.

"It turns out Mr. Yasumoto taught Mr. Kanehara his craft. Showed him everything—from how to extract the broth and boil the noodles just right, to the best way of seasoning the roast pork. But he was also very insistent that Mr. Kanehara should add his own personal touches. And so, drawing on his advice, Mr. Kanehara developed his own unique bowl of ramen."

"So that humble yatai owner was responsible for the success of Shinsen Kyoichi? Who'd have thought it!"

"Amazing, isn't it?" said Koishi, refilling his teacup.

"Now, consummate professional that he is, Mr. Kanehara could remember the recipe for Mr. Yasumoto's ramen right down to the last detail. He insisted it would taste just as good these days, no matter how much the world of ramen has changed in the meantime. Well, I cooked it just as he instructed—and this was the result." Nagare glanced down at the bowl, in which just a tiny puddle of broth remained.

"What a story." Katsuji reached for the bowl and slowly drank the last of the broth.

Nagare's expression became pensive. "You know, I reckon the most important thing Mr. Yasumoto passed on to Mr. Kanehara was a certain mindset: the desire to keep chasing that dream of his."

"By the way," said Koishi, "what happened to the other two members of your theater troupe?"

"Kunisue got a job at a major electrical appliance manufacturer," replied Katsuji, "but they laid him off when the economy crashed in the early nineties. He's worked at various middle-ranking companies since then, but he's never given up the amateur drama. Four or five times a year he puts on a show at some event space on the outskirts of Tokyo, but I have to admit I haven't been once. As for Yasaka, he became a professional actor, but five years ago he passed away without ever really making it."

"Meanwhile," said Nagare, "you were the first one to give up your dreams—and now look at you. The founder of a successful company."

Katsuji wordlessly twirled his teacup around in his hand.

"Now, I gave up on my own dreams a long while ago, so I'm hardly one to talk," continued Nagare, looking steadily at Katsuji. "But here's what I think. As long as you've really poured yourself into something—whether it's your job, or anything else in life—someone will always turn up to carry on where you left off."

"Carry *what* on, though?" said Katsuji, before continuing. "You know that old proverb, 'Spare no effort in youth, no matter the cost'? Well, there's another version of it."

Nagare cocked his head slightly. "What's that, then?"

"'Our youthful dreams are riches, never to be sold.'"

"Interesting. I'll have to store that one away in here," said Nagare, tapping a finger to his forehead.

"As if you'll remember! I'll write it down," said Koishi, scribbling the phrase in the margin of a newspaper.

"Don't bother," said Katsuji, grinning from ear to ear. "I made it up, actually."

"Well, you had me fooled," said Nagare, smiling. "Now, there's a copy of that recipe in here for you." He inserted a folder into a paper bag. "Mr. Kanehara thought you'd be able to get all the ingredients, even in Tokyo."

"Thank you. How much do I owe you?" said Katsuji, getting out his wallet. "For that meal the last time too."

"Just send whatever seems right to this account, please," said Koishi, handing him a slip of paper.

"I'll do it as soon as I get back," said Katsuji, sliding the slip into his wallet.

"Phew," said Nagare, sliding the door open. "It really is sweltering out here."

"Oh, I'd expect nothing less from Kyoto," replied Katsuji as he stepped outside. He was immediately accosted by Drowsy, who came rushing over.

"You'll ruin his suit," said Koishi, picking the cat up and cradling him in her arms.

"Thank you for everything." Katsuji bowed deeply, then set off down the street.

"Take care!" called Koishi, bowing in his direction, with Drowsy still clutched to her chest.

"Oh, Mr. Onodera!" called Nagare. Katsuji stopped and wheeled around to face them again. "About that troupe of yours . . ."

"What about it?"

"The name. Why the Hamsters?"

"Ham acting. Get it?"

"Ah." Nagare smiled. "I thought as much."

His face stretching into a grin, Katsuji turned and began walking again. Once he had disappeared from view, Koishi set Drowsy down and followed Nagare back inside.

"Do you think he'll change his mind?" asked Koishi. "About his son, I mean."

Nagare removed the towel from around his neck and sat down on one of the folding chairs. "Who knows? Maybe he will, and maybe he won't. In the end, does it matter?"

"What made you want to follow in *your* dad's footsteps, then?" asked Koishi, sitting down next to him.

"I wouldn't know," said Nagare curtly. "It was a long time ago."

"Did Grandpa force you into it?"

"No, not at all. He never put his foot down about anything, really. Well, maybe just the once."

"When was that?"

"When I first brought Kikuko to meet him and your grandma. He turned to me and said, 'You better look after her, you hear me?'"

"Huh," said Koishi, her gaze drifting toward the altar in the living room.

"I did just as he told me, too. Even if it wasn't for as long as we might have hoped." Nagare made his way into the living room, sat down in front of the altar, and adopted a praying pose.

"Hey, Mum, did he ever tell *you* that story?" said Koishi, kneeling next to him and lighting a stick of incense.

"Course I didn't," said Nagare, smiling sheepishly as he unclasped his hands.

"I guess some things are passed on even when they're left unsaid," murmured Koishi, her own hands still pressed together in prayer.

"I bought ingredients for gyoza tonight. Figured you'd want something to go with a drink before the ramen. Get the hot plate ready, would you? I need to rinse this sweat off."

"Gyoza! I can't wait. Do you think we have enough beer?" said Koishi, getting up to look in the fridge.

"Don't worry—I asked Hiroshi to bring us over a case. He should be here with it any minute."

"Brilliant. We'll have to make enough gyoza for three, then," said Koishi, rolling up her sleeves.

"Four, you mean," said Nagare, glancing back over his shoulder at the altar. "Kikuko would be furious if we forgot hers."

Chapter 6

Ten-don

1

According to the lunar calendar, spring was just around the corner; but it was still only early February, and a wintry chill permeated the air. As Keiko Fujikawa passed through the ticket barriers at Kyoto station, a gust of icy wind stole the wide-brimmed hat from her head, sending her scurrying after it.

It was true what she'd heard, then: the winters here were even fiercer than in her northern hometown of Ishinomaki. Despite her black leather gloves, her fingers were soon numb from the biting cold. Keiko blew into her hands to warm them, pulled the brim of her hat down over her eyes, and ventured out of the station.

She wore a thick gray coat and fur scarf. *Really nailed the old-lady look, haven't I*, thought Keiko, who had turned fifty the previous year. With a map in one hand, she turned north up the long straight avenue of Karasuma-dori. Of all the pedestrians she passed, only one seemed to notice that they had just walked past Keiko Fujikawa—and that couldn't just be because of the sunglasses she was wearing. No, she thought to herself, by now she must have all but disappeared from the collective memory.

Soon after crossing Shichijo-dori, she turned right onto Shomen-dori, heading east until she reached the building she was looking for.

"*This* place?" she murmured, removing her sunglasses and gazing up at the mortar wall of the two-story building.

There was no sign above the door; it looked for all the world like a private residence. But the enticing smells that came wafting into the street were enough to convince her that this was, indeed, a restaurant.

She slid open the door and was immediately confronted by the puzzled face of Koishi Kamogawa.

"Can we help you?"

"I'm here for the food detective service," said Keiko, removing her gloves and glancing around the interior.

"Oh, you're one of *those*! Go on, take a seat." Koishi slid the silver tray she was holding under one arm and pulled out one of the folding chairs.

"Thank you." Keiko set her black tote bag on the table, then got out her phone.

Koishi bustled about, clearing the dishes on the counter

onto her tray. Keiko glanced sideways at her, then went back to swiping away at her phone.

"Will you be eating first?" asked Koishi as she wiped down the counter.

Keiko looked up from her phone. "What are you serving?"

"First-time customers get the set menu," said Nagare Kamogawa, emerging from the kitchen.

"Hello there," said Keiko, half rising from her seat to bow.

"Welcome," said Nagare. There was a pause while he studied her face from the side as though caught up in vague recognition. Then he gathered himself. "So . . . would you like something to eat?"

Keiko smiled faintly and put a hand to her stomach. "All I had before I left Tokyo this morning was a slice of toast."

"Is there anything you don't like?"

"Oh, I'll eat anything," replied Keiko, tucking her phone into her bag.

"Well, you're in luck. I had a very demanding customer in earlier, so I've prepared all sorts of dishes. Hopefully you'll enjoy it—especially if you've come all the way from Tokyo. Just give me a moment." Nagare darted off to the kitchen.

As the faint fragrance of dashi stock came wafting into the deserted restaurant, a loud grumble issued from Keiko's stomach, breaking the silence that had fallen over the room. Reflexively putting a hand to her belly once more, she glanced around anxiously to see if anyone had heard.

"So, how did you find us, then?" asked Koishi, who had finished cleaning and now came over to stand by the table.

With a relieved look, Keiko reached into her bag and produced a magazine. "I read about you in here."

"Ah, *Gourmet Monthly.*" Koishi tilted her head slightly to one side. "But our ad doesn't specify an address, does it?"

"Akane Daidoji told me where to go," Keiko said with a smile.

"Oh, you know Akane?"

"Yes. We first worked together five years or so ago."

"Do you work in the media, then?" asked Koishi, studying Keiko's features.

"Something like that." Another faint smile flickered at the corners of Keiko's mouth.

"Ooh, lucky you! It must be so glamorous."

Keiko shrugged. "So people seem to think."

She glanced around the restaurant once more. No menu, and nothing resembling a cash register. There was a doorway on either side of the long counter; the one on the right was obscured by a noren curtain. Whenever Koishi or Nagare brushed it to one side, she caught a glimpse of an elegant Buddhist altar set into the wall of the tatami room beyond. It really was a quite peculiar restaurant, thought Keiko, furrowing her brow in confusion.

"Sorry for the wait," said Nagare, appearing with a black lacquered tray, which he set on the table.

"I'm sure it'll be worth it," replied Keiko, sitting up in her chair.

"What can I get you to drink?" asked Koishi. "Maybe some sake to warm you up a little?"

"Go on, then." Keiko smiled. "Seeing as I'm here."

"Koishi," said Nagare, "there's a bottle of Tanikaze in the fridge upstairs. Warm that up for her, will you? In the Shigaraki bottle." Koishi nodded and hurried off.

"You have Tanikaze?" asked Keiko, her eyes widening.

"I like my sumo, see. Couldn't resist the idea of a sake named after a famous wrestler from up north. This might be heresy, but I think even a premium daiginjo like that tastes rather nice warmed up. Rounds the flavor out nicely." With this, Nagare made his way back into the kitchen—just as Koishi reappeared with the ceramic sake bottle.

"I warmed it up in a pot of hot water, but let me know if you'd like it a little hotter."

Keiko touched the bottle and smiled. "That feels perfect."

"It's especially cold today, so I thought I'd serve you some dishes that are still warm," said Nagare, arriving with a straw pot stand, which he set on her tray.

Keiko reached for the Shigaraki bottle and filled her Oribe sake cup. "I thought I was ready for the Kyoto winter, but it really is something else, isn't it?"

"They do say the cold bites in a different way down here," said Nagare, smiling as he set a lidded, round-handled earthenware pan on the pot stand.

Keiko took her first sip from the cup, then let out a deep sigh. "Delicious sake."

"I've tried to include a little bit of everything that's good to eat at this time of year," said Nagare, lifting the lid from the large, shallow pan. "Starting in the top left: fugu from Mikawa Bay, fried karaage style, and boiled Kano crab. To the right of that are grilled skewers of duck meatball and Kujo green onion, and tilefish tempura. Shogoin daikon and millet cake, baked in a miso glaze; Horikawa burdock and hamo fish cakes in broth. Below that are sake-steamed hamaguri clams, stewed Kintoki carrots and Kujo green onion, and the grilled fish is miso-marinated pomfret. There are heated stones at the bottom of the pan, so watch you don't burn yourself."

As Keiko listened, her eyes darted around the pan.

Already gripping her chopsticks, she nodded along to Nagare's every word.

"I don't know where to start. Is there some kind of order I'm supposed to eat this in?"

"Not in the slightest. Eat whatever you feel like, in whatever order you like. Now, enjoy!" Nagare made his way back into the kitchen.

"Let me know if you need a top-up of that sake, okay?" said Koishi, before following him.

Keiko leaned in close to the pan and took a deep sniff.

"How fragrant!" she exclaimed.

She decided to start with the tilefish tempura. She sprinkled a piece with some of the accompanying matcha salt, popped it into her mouth, and closed her eyes. After chewing a few times, her cheeks creased into a smile.

"Delicious."

Next she sampled the miso-glazed daikon radish, the deep-fried fugu, and the pomfret—each of which earned from Keiko a grin and a nod.

"All to your liking?" asked Nagare, arriving at her side again. He was carrying a silver tray on which various small plates were arranged.

"Everything is fantastic—really."

"Here are a few palate cleansers. Filet of baby sea bream, vinegared and wrapped in thinly sliced Shogoin turnip. The grilled fish is moroko, marinated in a spicy

181

sauce. And those are sweet-simmered black soybeans. Just let me know if you'd like some rice to go with it—today's is cooked with sardines."

"Do you suppose I could . . . have another bottle of sake?" asked Keiko, picking up the ceramic bottle by its neck.

"Of course," said Nagare, taking it from her and hurrying back into the kitchen.

Next, Keiko reached for one of the skewers, held it sideways alongside her mouth, and took a bite. Juice oozed from one of the duck meatballs and went dribbling down her chin. Panicking slightly, she retrieved a handkerchief from her bag and carefully wiped it away.

"This sake packs quite a punch," said Nagare as he appeared with a fresh bottle and refilled her cup. "I hope it's not overpowering the food?"

Keiko smiled and took a sip. "Not at all. They're evenly matched!"

"Now, we should probably talk about this dish you're looking for. Shall I bring that rice through in a moment, so you can finish off here?"

"Please," said Keiko, lining her fingers up on the table.

The restaurant fell silent again; for a moment, all that could be heard was the trickling of sake from bottle to cup. Keiko, feeling her mood lighten, looked up at the ceiling and closed her eyes.

A single star in the winter sky—
Twinkling just for me.

She half hummed the words, her voice so quiet as to be almost inaudible, yet inflected with a slight vibrato. The lyrics seemed to well up from somewhere deep inside her.

One of the sweet black soybeans slipped from her chopsticks and onto the table. Flustered, she picked it up with her fingers and popped it into her mouth.

Just as she began crunching away at the pickled turnip, Nagare arrived again, this time bearing a clay pot, from which he began spooning rice into a small bowl.

"Grilled sardines. We eat them at this time of year—you know, for Setsubun, to ward off bad fortune. Afterward, you're supposed to spear the heads of the fishes on a holly branch and hang them by your front door. Scares the demons right off, apparently." He set the bowl of rice in front of Keiko.

"Where I'm from, we do the usual bean throwing, but I don't remember ever eating sardines for Setsubun!" She sniffed the bowl. "Smells fabulous."

"I'll leave the pot here, so help yourself to seconds. I'll just fetch the soup," said Nagare, returning to the kitchen.

Keiko had an uncommon fondness for sardines and other blue-backed fish, and she began enthusiastically shoveling the rice dish down. The fragrance of the finely chopped perilla and sesame only heightened her appetite. In no time at all, she had emptied the bowl and was reaching for the round spatula that Nagare had left in the pot of rice.

"Sardine dumpling soup," said Nagare, returning with a lacquered Negoro bowl. "Plenty of grated ginger and yuzu in there too. Should warm you right up." He removed the lid, unleashing a cloud of citrus-fragranced steam. Keiko's eyes widened.

"I love my sardines, you know. This rice is just divine," she said, refilling her bowl to the brim.

"Very pleased to hear it! Finish the whole pot if you can. There should be some nice crispy bits at the bottom." Nagare peered into the pot, then retreated to the kitchen once more.

Keiko held the soup bowl to her lips, then quietly took a sip. The sharp scent of the yuzu tickled her nostrils. She closed her eyes, bit into one of the sardine dumplings—and all of a sudden was overcome by a vision of the sea off the coast of Ishinomaki. Nostalgia for her hometown seemed to ripple outward from her mouth, slowly radiating through her entire body. Her eyes began to glisten.

After a moment's hesitation, she scraped the bottom of the pot with the spatula and transferred the last of the sardine rice to her bowl. When she had polished that off,

Keiko pressed her palms together in gratitude, then set her chopsticks down.

"You look like you could manage another bowl," remarked Nagare, reappearing at her side with a Tokoname-ware teapot. "I should have made more rice."

Keiko rubbed her stomach. "Oh, I've had plenty. It was all just so delicious. I'm stuffed!"

"I'm glad you enjoyed it," said Nagare. He looked down at the empty pot, then beamed at Keiko. "And that you're such a thorough eater!"

"Akane did tell me you were a good cook, but that was something else."

"Been gossiping about me again, has she? She does like to exaggerate." Nagare gave a self-conscious smile, then changed the topic. "Koishi's waiting in the office. Shall I show you through?"

"Ah, yes. Almost forgot what I came here for." Keiko sipped down the rest of her tea, then got to her feet.

"Hope I didn't rush you," said Nagare as he led Keiko down the corridor to the office. She followed close behind, gazing in fascination at the photographs plastered all over the walls.

"Did you make all these yourself?"

"I like a challenge, you see," said Nagare, turning and smiling. "If I'm asked to make something, I always give it my best shot."

Keiko stopped to inspect one of the photos in particular. "This sushi looks fantastic."

"Ah," said Nagare, also coming to a halt. "Sardine sushi roll. Marinated in vinegar, a bit like mackerel sushi. You really do like your sardines, don't you?"

"My father was a fisherman," said Keiko with a distant smile, "so I had to eat the things almost every day when I was little. Couldn't stand them back then, mind!"

"That's often the way, isn't it?" said Nagare, walking again. "You hate something as a kid, then grow up to love it. Our palate is a mysterious thing."

Nagare opened the door to reveal Koishi waiting inside the office.

"Hello again," said Keiko, walking in and perching hesitantly on the end of the sofa.

Koishi grinned at her. "You can sit in the middle if you like, you know."

"Sorry. I'm feeling a little self-conscious," said Keiko, shuffling along the sofa.

"Would you mind filling this form out?" asked Koishi, sliding her clipboard across the table. Keiko placed it on her lap and began scribbling away. After a moment, her hand froze.

"If there's something you'd rather not write, then don't worry—you can skip that part," said Koishi.

"It's not that," replied Keiko, the corners of her lips curling upward. "Can you believe it? I forgot my own date of birth for a moment. Getting old is a scary business, I tell you." She handed the clipboard back to Koishi.

"Keiko Fujikawa. Occupation: music industry. Sorry, I said 'the media' earlier, didn't I?"

"Oh, it's all much of a muchness."

"And you live in Shinjuku, Tokyo. All skyscrapers around there, isn't it? I bet it looks stunning at night."

"I don't know. It can be hard to enjoy the scenery on your own," sighed Keiko. "Makes you sad, if anything."

"You never married, then?"

"Oh no. Never had much luck in that area."

Koishi nodded deeply. "That makes two of us."

"You're still young. It's a little different when you're my age."

"What do you mean? You don't look a day over fifty."

Keiko tilted her head to one side and smiled. "You're just being nice. But thank you."

"Now, shall we get down to business?" said Koishi, leaning forward. "What dish are you looking for?"

"Ten-don."

"As in, tempura served over a bowl of rice? Not many places serve it in Kyoto. I guess Tokyoites really do have different tastes."

"Actually, I'm not from Tokyo," said Keiko, gazing evenly at Koishi. "I grew up in Ishinomaki, up north. I moved to the capital when I was twenty, and that was where I had the ten-don. I'd never eaten anything like it."

"Could you tell me a bit more about it?" asked Koishi, opening up her notebook and readying her pen.

"I'd been in Tokyo for just over a year at the time. The head of my agency took me out for a celebratory meal when things were going well for me. It was a restaurant in Asakusa."

"Do you know what it was called?"

"Tenfusa, I think the name was."

"And it's not in business anymore?"

"If it was, I wouldn't be here, would I?"

The two exchanged a look and laughed.

"True. So, what was so special about it?" asked Koishi.

"The tempura was tasty enough, but it was the sauce that really blew me away. Full-bodied, I suppose you might call it. Sweet and salty at the same time—and yet somehow not too heavy."

"I thought ten-don was basically the same everywhere you go. You know, all smothered with that dark, gloopy sauce—the kind of thing you'd never get past a Kyotoite."

"No, this place was different. I tried the ten-don at a few famous tempura places after that, but none of them hit the spot. It was something about the flavor."

Koishi folded her arms and cocked her head. "Do you remember anything a little more specific? Dad's the one who does the detective work, you see, and I have a feeling he'll need a bit more to go on."

"The tempura was prawn, conger eel, some kind of white-fleshed fish. . . ." said Keiko, gazing up at the ceiling as she retraced her memories. "Green peppers and nori. There was nothing unusual about the batter that I can recall, either. But the sauce wasn't as dark as you seem to be imagining. I think it was a bit lighter than at other places."

Koishi's pen was scratching away. "So there was nothing unusual about the tempura itself—it was the sauce that was distinctive."

"Oh, and the soup that came with it! It was really tast—" Keiko suddenly broke off.

"Are you okay?" asked Koishi with a concerned look.

"That soup I had just now. It tasted similar somehow. A sort of nostalgic . . ." Keiko shook her head. "No, that's impossible. It wasn't a sardine soup they served at the tempura place. I must be imagining things." She seemed to be trying to convince herself of this.

"Do you remember the precise location of the restaurant? Asakusa is a pretty big area."

"It was in the area behind Sensoji temple, if I recall correctly. Down a narrow street. I think there was a sushi restaurant next door."

"If it was so delicious, why did you never go back?" asked Koishi, making a slightly impatient expression. "You were living in Shinjuku. Couldn't you have just popped over to Asakusa whenever you pleased?"

"My manager told me he'd take me again when I had my next big break, so I suppose I was just waiting for that day to come. It felt like it might be bad luck to do otherwise, somehow." Keiko sighed, her gaze dropping to the low table in front of her.

"Well, I'm sure Dad'll be able to track this ten-don of yours down."

Keiko looked up again. "Really? Thank you very much."

Koishi closed her notebook, then opened it again. "Tell me. What made you want to eat it again after all this time?"

"Well, my parents are getting on in years, and I'm thinking it might be time to head back to Ishinomaki so I can look after them. But before I leave Tokyo, I want to eat that ten-don one last time."

"And then you'll be able to return home in peace," said Koishi, nodding.

"Oh, and if I can learn how to make it myself, I thought I could make it for my parents. You see, right after I ate it the first time, I called them up. I couldn't help myself—I just had to let them know about the delights that were on offer in Tokyo. I told them to visit me the next time things went well for me—that I'd treat them to the meal of their lives." Keiko chuckled and shrugged. "Then, before I knew it, three whole decades went by."

"I see," said Koishi, closing her notebook again with an air of finality. "Well, I'll make sure Dad gets right on the case."

"I appreciate it," said Keiko, getting to her feet and bowing.

"Did that all go smoothly?" asked Nagare, looking up from his newspaper in the restaurant.

"Koishi was very patient," said Keiko. "I'm afraid my memory is a little hazy. I hope I'm not asking too much!" She bowed deeply in his direction.

Nagare got to his feet and looked steadily at her. "Whatever it is you're looking for, I'll leave no stone unturned. That's a promise."

Keiko pulled on her coat and grabbed her bag, and made her way out of the restaurant. A tabby cat came padding over to greet her.

"What a charming creature!" she exclaimed, tickling the animal's jaw. "What's its name?"

"Drowsy," replied Koishi. "The poor thing isn't allowed in the restaurant—even on a freezing day like this!" She shot Nagare a reproving look.

Nagare scowled back at her. "What, you expect me to let that ball of fur in here while people are trying to eat their food?"

Keiko smiled as she scooped Drowsy up in her arms. "Back home in Ishinomaki, the streets are full of cats."

"I suppose there must be all that delicious fish for them to eat," said Nagare.

"That's right. They have a knack for finding the freshest, tastiest fish in town."

"Pretty discerning creatures, aren't they? I guess there's a reason people say a spoiled fish is 'one for the cats to pass on.'"

"Oh yes. One sniff"—Keiko did her best impression of a cat smelling a fish—"and if they don't like it, they're out of there!"

"Erm, about next time," said Koishi, interrupting their banter. "Can you come back in two weeks?"

"Fine by me." Keiko nodded. "But will *you* have

enough time?" She turned to Nagare. He seemed to hesitate for a moment, then smiled.

"I'll manage."

"Oh, how could I forget! I haven't paid for my meal." Keiko set Drowsy down and reached for her purse.

"No need. You can pay for everything later, all at once."

"All right, then," replied Keiko, glancing at them each in turn. "I'll be looking forward to it." She turned and set off down Shomen-dori the way she'd come.

"Take care!" called Koishi after her.

After she'd gone, Nagare glared at the cat again. "Hey, you—no sneaking inside!"

"Poor thing," said Koishi, sliding the door closed behind them. "It's so cold today. He just wants to be somewhere warm!"

"What's the dish?" asked Nagare, settling at one of the tables.

"Ten-don."

"Huh. I wouldn't have guessed."

"Because of her age, you mean?"

"No. I just assumed Keiko Fujikawa would be the type to pick a fancy seafood dinner or something."

"Wait," said Koishi, her eyes widening. She retracted the notebook she had been holding out, clutching it to her chest instead. "How do you know her name?"

"Know her name? She's Keiko Fujikawa—anyone can see that! Don't tell me you didn't recognize her."

"What, is she famous?"

"I suppose she *was* before your time. Bit of a one-hit wonder too. It's sad, really."

Nagare took the notebook from Koishi and began flicking through it.

"Let's see," said Koishi. "Keiko Fujikawa. Music industry . . . Oh, is she a singer? It's starting to ring a bell. . . . What did she sing?" She furrowed her brow and rubbed her temples as she tried to remember.

"'Lonely Star,'" murmured Nagare as he leafed through the notebook.

"What's it about?"

"Her lover has died, and she imagines him watching over her like a star in the sky. Sad old tune, really."

"I'll have to google it later," said Koishi, putting on her apron and making her way into the kitchen.

Nagare, meanwhile, had propped his chin in his hand and was looking through Koishi's notes. As he riffled through the pages, he sang quietly to himself.

"Because I know you're watching from on high . . ."

"Oh, that one!" said Koishi, peering through the curtain that hung over the door to the kitchen. "You sing that in the bath sometimes."

"Never mind that," said Nagare hurriedly, as if to hide his embarrassment. "What's this you've written about 'Dad's soup,' eh?"

"Oh, you can erase that part. She mentioned something about how that soup you served her tasted similar to the one that came with this ten-don of hers. But then she changed her mind. Said she must be getting confused." Koishi lowered the curtain.

The restaurant was deathly silent, the way it only got in the depths of winter. The only sound was the occasional clatter from the kitchen, where Koishi was washing the dishes.

Nagare appeared to be deep in thought, his gaze still fixed on the notebook. Then, with a sip of his tea, he clapped the notebook shut.

"I'm off to Tokyo."

"Ooh, the big city! Can I come too?" Koishi had emerged from the kitchen with an excited gleam in her eyes.

"You'll only slow me down," he chuckled. "Anyway, your mother'll get lonely if we leave her here on her own."

"What if I brought her photo with us? We could all go together."

"Hmm. That's not a bad idea. There's a sushi place she loved in Asakusa, you know. Shall we take her there?"

"Oh, perfect. Let's do it, Dad."

Nagare blushed as Koishi hugged him. "Just so we're clear, I'm not paying your expenses."

Koishi turned toward the back room and cupped one ear. "What's that, Mum? 'Stingy old codger,' did you say?"

"Oh, she's one to talk! Remember the pittance she used to dole out to me as spending money?"

With a wry grin, Nagare glanced out the window. Since they'd come inside, a fine layer of snow had settled over the street.

2

Stepping out of the station and onto Karasuma-dori, Keiko stopped to gaze up at Kyoto Tower, glowing against the evening sky. The wind on her cheeks felt ever so slightly warmer than last time. She yanked down the zipper on her coat, then made her way across the junction.

Striding along, her head held high, she arrived at the restaurant sooner than she'd been expecting. She was greeted by Drowsy, who hurried over and began frolicking around at her feet.

"Hello, you," she said, squatting to stroke the cat. "Poor thing. Nippy today, isn't it?"

The door slid open to reveal Koishi. "Hello! You'd better come in from the cold."

"It's an improvement on last time, at least. Look, no gloves!"

Keiko made her way inside, removed her coat, and combed her fingers through her hair.

The fragrant aroma of sesame oil filled the restaurant. As she slid her coat onto the rack in the corner, Keiko's nose began to twitch.

Nagare appeared from the kitchen and removed his white chef's hat. "Thanks for coming back. It took me a while, but I think I've got it just right."

"Dad's been frying tempura day and night," said Koishi. She peered out the door at the cat outside. "Drowsy loves the smell. He's been sitting hopefully by the door the whole time."

"Thanks for all the effort." Keiko bowed at them each in turn.

"It'll be ready very soon. Just give me a moment," said Nagare, hastening back to the kitchen.

"Can I get you some tea?" asked Koishi. "Or maybe something stronger?"

"I'll stick to tea today," replied Keiko with a smile. "I want to keep my taste buds fresh for the main dish!"

Koishi bowed slightly, then poured the tea from her

Banko-ware teapot. "I'm really sorry about last time. I had no idea you were so famous."

"Oh, don't worry about it. It's only natural for someone your age to have never heard of me."

"I didn't make the connection at first, but I do know 'Lonely Star.' Dad's always singing it in the bath!"

Keiko sipped her tea and smiled gently. "I'm very happy to hear that."

"Koishi, it's almost ready!" called Nagare from the kitchen.

Koishi hurriedly set a chopstick stand on the table, together with a pair of disposable chopsticks. "Tempura is always best freshly fried, isn't it?"

"I can't wait," said Keiko, half rising in order to pull her chair forward slightly.

"Here you go." Nagare arrived at Keiko's side with a round vermilion-lacquered tray. On it was a deep, blue-and-white porcelain donburi bowl, its contents obscured by a lid.

"It smells wonderful," said Keiko, her eyes glazing over dreamily.

"I'll bring the soup through in a moment. First, the ten-don." Nagare removed the lid. Steam rose up from the bowl in thin wisps. Keiko pressed her palms together in appreciation, then reached for the chopsticks. Nagare and Koishi retreated to the kitchen.

Keiko cupped the donburi bowl in the palm of her hand, sat up straight, and brought one of the pieces of prawn tempura to her mouth.

It was a kuruma prawn, about the size of a middle finger. As she bit into it, a pleasant sweetness filled her mouth. With the taste still lingering, she reached for a green pepper, also coated in batter, which she followed with a mouthful of the sauce-infused rice. After the second mouthful or so, an excited look came into Keiko's eyes.

"The taste," she murmured to herself. "The fragrance . . . It's exactly the same!" Setting the bowl back down on the table, she scrabbled in her bag for her handkerchief. She blotted it to her cheek just in time to catch the first tears.

Smiling to herself, she set the handkerchief on her lap, then reached for the bowl once more.

This time, she separated the strip of conger eel into two halves, then inserted the first of them into her mouth. The second she accompanied with a mouthful of rice. Now she broke into another, even broader smile, one that chased the tears from her face, before devouring the entire piece of white-fleshed fish, right down to its little tail. All that was left now was the rice—and the sheets of nori, which she used to scoop up every last grain in the bowl.

"Did I get it right?" said Nagare, arriving with a black lacquered bowl on his silver tray.

"Oh yes," replied Keiko, looking up at him. "It was exactly how I remembered it."

"Good!"

She flashed him an embarrassed grin. "It was so tasty that I've gone and polished it off before the soup even got here."

"Ah, but I was hoping you would. I mean, that was only a small serving of rice I gave you! Take a breather, enjoy the soup, and then I'll bring you some seconds, all right?" Nagare transferred her rice bowl to his tray, then set the bowl of soup in front of her.

"Oh my. You're going to fry a whole second batch just for me?"

"Wouldn't want you eating anything but freshly fried tempura, would we?" said Nagare, smiling over his shoulder as he made his way back to the kitchen.

Keiko removed the lid from the bowl, savored the fragrant steam that came billowing out from underneath, then took her first sip.

The transparent broth had a delicate flavor that contrasted with the richly flavored ten-don. As she bit into the large fish ball in the center of the bowl, the smell of the sea seemed to fill her nostrils. Then, as she slurped down some of the accompanying mitsuba stems together with more of the broth, she felt as though she'd been transported back to land. The flavors were all incredibly subtle. When she'd finished around half the bowl, Keiko carefully replaced the lid.

"Ready for the second round?" asked Nagare, setting down a fresh bowl of ten-don.

Keiko blushed slightly. "I know you said these were small portions, but this still feels very indulgent! I feel like a youngster again."

"Well, I can always make you a third bowl!" The two looked at each other and grinned.

"This second portion," said Keiko, removing the lid and inspecting the contents with a curious expression. "It *is* the same as the first, isn't it?"

"You just tuck in, okay? I'll bring you some more tea."

Once Nagare had returned to the kitchen, Keiko positioned the bowl in her hand just as she had the first time, then took a deep sniff. The fragrance was the same . . . and yet, somehow, undoubtedly, different. She tried a bite of the kuruma prawn and a mouthful of the sauce-soaked rice, and divided the eel into two once more. Carefully savoring the taste of each piece of tempura, she slowly chewed away, occasionally pausing for another sip of the soup. She finished off the sardine ball, then returned to the ten-don. This second portion was just as delicious as the first. It was the flavor of the soup that seemed to have changed—and yet it was the same bowl. She alternated between the soup and the ten-don, wondering why on earth that should be, until in no time at all, both the bowls in front of her were empty.

"That's what I like to see," said Nagare, pouring her some hojicha from a Kyo-ware teapot.

Keiko bowed in appreciation. "I'm nice and full. All nostalgia aside, that was absolutely delicious."

"Glad to hear it," said Nagare, nodding.

"How on earth did you manage it?" asked Keiko, cupping her Shigaraki-ware teacup in both hands.

Koishi arrived from the kitchen, hugging a transparent file to her chest. "Another one of his field investigations. That's always the way with Dad! I decided to go with him—you know, to keep him company."

Nagare pulled a face as he snatched the file from her. "She insisted. Slowed me right down."

"Hey! If it wasn't for me, you'd have gone the wrong way on the metro."

Appearing not to hear her, Nagare turned to Keiko. "You were right about the name of the restaurant. Ten-fusa, in Asakusa. It closed down twelve years ago. This is the place, right?" He opened up the file and showed her a photo.

"Yes," said Keiko, leaning forward. "That's just how I remember it!"

"I borrowed these photos from the manager of the shopping arcade it was on," continued Nagare, flipping through the file. "The owner of Tenfusa was from Ichinomiya, over in the Kazusa area of Chiba. The sushi place next door, Fusa Sushi, was run by his younger brother. That 'fusa' in their names must be a nod to Kazusa, seeing as you'd write it using the same character."

"My manager was from Chiba too. Tateyama, to be precise. I wonder if there was some sort of connection."

"Twelve years ago, when the owner of Tenfusa passed away from illness, his younger brother decided to fold up his business too. He went back to Kazusa and started a new restaurant with the same name: Fusa Sushi. The shopping arcade manager found out the address for me—and off we went to Chiba." Nagare settled into the chair opposite Keiko and unfolded a map on the table.

"He almost got on the wrong train that time too," said Koishi, giving Keiko an amused look.

"Don't interrupt," snapped Nagare. "Now, the specialty at Fusa Sushi is called Kazusa-meshi. Apparently it dates back to the restaurant's Tokyo days."

"Kazusa-meshi?" repeated Keiko.

"Tell me, have you heard of Fukagawa-meshi?"

"You mean the rice dish with asari clams on top?"

"That's the one. Kazusa-meshi is the same thing, but using hamaguri clams instead—and it's one of the most popular items on the menu. The Kazusa area's famous for hamaguri, after all. These days, people line up around the block to try it."

Keiko looked puzzled. "But what's the connection with the ten-don?"

"Kazusa-meshi is a pretty simple dish," said Nagare, searching through the file for a photo of it. "You quickly simmer the hamaguri clams in sake, mirin, and soy sauce, then serve them on the rice. At Fusa Sushi, the resulting leftover liquid was boiled down and used as a glaze for the conger eel and hamaguri clam sushi. But because Kazusa-meshi was so popular, there was still plenty of the stuff left over. Rather than waste it, the owner started taking it over to his brother next door—who put it in his ten-don sauce. The owner of Fusa Sushi kindly told me the recipe."

"So that sauce I just ate was flavored with . . . hamaguri clams?" asked Keiko, gazing steadily at the photo.

"That's right. Now, the soup at Tenfusa was hamaguri broth. I made the fish ball the way he told me too, using a mix of hamaguri and white-fleshed fish. That's right—the first time you visited, I happened to be serving a sake-simmered hamaguri stock for the soup. Of course, in that soup, the fish balls were made from sardines—which your hometown of Ishinomaki is famous for. That, combined with the clam-flavored broth, explains why you found the flavor so nostalgic. You've quite the discerning palate, clearly!"

Keiko had fallen silent. In her mind, she could almost hear the hands of a clock turning backward.

"The tempura was fried in a seventy-thirty mix of sesame oil and salad oil. That gives it a slightly thicker crust. What you use for the batter itself isn't too important—practically anything will do. The sauce for the donburi wasn't too tricky, either. I've scribbled a rough recipe down for you, so you should be able to make it for your parents."

Nagare set the file down on the table. Keiko reached for it and began scanning its pages.

"My father's always telling me not to come home until I've scored another hit. But my mother says singing isn't everything in life, and I should come home whenever I feel like it. I've always felt so torn." Keiko lifted her gaze toward the ceiling.

"Sounds like, in their own way, they each wanted the best for you," said Nagare, also looking into the distance.

"Somehow, thirty years have gone by, and all I have to show for it is that one song." Keiko wiped the corner of her eye with a little finger. "What an idiot I've been."

"Listen," said Nagare with a kind smile. "I'm no expert on these matters, but it seems to me that *how many* songs you put out isn't what's important. Sure, it might just be one song to you, but to all your fans, it's a precious gift. That one song has helped all sorts of people through tough times. It's given them the strength to go on. I know that much because I'm one of them."

Hearing this, Keiko couldn't help remembering the altar she had glimpsed in the back room.

"I'll dry my tears—I'll wait for tomorrow to pass by . . ." sang Koishi with a smile. "See, he sings it in the bath so often that even I've learned the words."

"Because I know you're watching from on high—always watching from on high," sang Keiko, finishing the line.

"Wow. The genuine article!" exclaimed Koishi, clapping her hands.

"Thank you both for everything. But I'm still not sure I've found my answer," said Keiko, smiling as she dabbed at her eyes with her handkerchief.

"Well, I'm not sure anyone ever does."

Keiko felt Nagare's words reverberate inside her.

"At least Dad got the ten-don right," said Koishi, refilling Keiko's teacup. "When I tried it myself, I wasn't convinced. The flavor was so sharp—not at all what I was expecting."

Keiko sipped her tea. "I suppose in this part of the country ten-don is a slightly milder affair."

"That's right," added Nagare. "Less gloopy too."

"Well, thank you very much," said Keiko, pulling her purse from her bag. "How much do I owe you—including for last time?"

"Just transfer whatever feels right to this account," said Koishi, handing her the usual slip of paper.

"All right. I'll do it as soon as I get the chance." Keiko carefully tucked the slip into her purse, then slid open the door to the restaurant.

Outside, Keiko was accosted once again by the cat.

"Drowsy, you lucky thing!" she exclaimed, scooping him up into her arms. "Something tells me you'll be getting some tasty leftovers later."

"Actually, Dad never gives him fried food, even though it's his favorite. Says it'll make him obese. Poor Drowsy!" Koishi looked moodily at her father.

"You can see why I'd worry, can't you?" retorted Nagare. "I mean, all he does is sleep all day."

"Oh, come on—we all need spoiling from time to time," said Keiko as she set the cat back down. "I mean, it's not like *I* eat ten-don every day, either."

"Hear, hear!" said Koishi.

Keiko bowed, thanked them again, then made her way

off down Shomen-dori. As Nagare and Koishi watched her go, Drowsy came over and sprawled at their feet instead.

Keiko stopped and turned. "Actually, *about* that ten-don . . ."

"What is it?" asked Nagare, stepping forward.

"When you gave me that second portion, something tasted different somehow."

"That's right. For your second bowl, I made a different sauce, instead of the clam-based one. Nostalgia's all well and good, but we shouldn't be afraid to try something new."

Keiko looked at him thoughtfully.

"Even if the tempura stays exactly the same," continued Nagare, looking steadily at her, "just switching up the other flavors can make it feel like a whole new dish. We're funny old creatures when it comes to food."

"I'll remember that. Thank you again." Keiko bowed deeply, then strode off down the street.

"Take care!" called Nagare to the figure receding into the evening. Koishi stood by his side, waving.

"It's so *cold*," said Koishi, hunching over and rubbing her hands. "Let's get back inside."

"Your posture's terrible, you know," replied Nagare, warily eyeing Drowsy as he opened the door. "You should take a leaf out of Keiko's book. See how she walked off with her head held high?"

"She did seem different today," said Koishi, sliding the door shut behind them. "Like a changed woman."

"Being reunited with your old flame will do that. Even if the old flame in question is a bowl of tempura," said Nagare as he made his way into the back room.

"Hey, Mum!" called Koishi to the altar as she followed him. "Did you hear what Dad said just now? 'Nostalgia's all well and good, but we shouldn't be afraid to try something new.'"

Nagare settled in front of the altar and lit a stick of incense. "I wasn't talking about Kikuko. She's a special case."

"Ten-don for dinner tonight, then?" asked Koishi, sitting behind him.

"Not *just* ten-don. I've got some oysters, flathead fish, and bay scallops in. Thought we could fry them up at the table with a drink."

"Great idea! But we're out of gas canisters for the stove." Koishi looked pleadingly at Nagare.

"Looks like I'll just have to pop out and get one, then."

Nagare pulled on a puffer jacket and slipped out of the restaurant.

The famous Mount Hiei wind was blowing down from the east. Nagare shivered and stuffed his hands into his jacket pockets.

Night had fallen, and puddles of warm light spilled from the windows lining the street. He could hear what sounded like a family sitting down for a meal. Blowing white puffs of breath into the air, Nagare gazed up at the night sky and, in a low voice, began to sing.

A single star in the winter sky—
Twinkling just for me.
I'll dry my tears, I'll wait for tomorrow to pass by.
Because I know you're watching from on high—
Always watching from on high.

Drowsy was sitting a short distance down the street. Just then, as if he'd been waiting for Nagare to finish, he looked up, yawned, and gave a single, soft *meow*.